ODD WOMAN OUT

BY THE SAME AUTHOR

ODD WOMAN OUT

Julian Fane

Book Guild Publishing
Sussex, England

First published in Great Britain in 2006 by
The Book Guild Ltd
25 High Street
Lewes, East Sussex
BN7 2LU

Typesetting in Garamond by
Keyboard Services, Luton, Bedfordshire

Printed in Great Britain by
Antony Rowe Ltd, Chippenham, Wiltshire

A catalogue record for this book is available from
The British Library

ISBN 1 84624 043 3

CONTENTS

PROLOGUE

The twentieth century – peace after two world wars – London in summer in the 1950s – the small hours of morning.

Moonlight in Pimlico Road, and an open-top two seater with the hood down. A man in the driving seat, his passenger female, a girl with short blonde hair. He wears a white shirt, black bow-tie, dinner jacket with lapels of satin that reflect light, she a white party dress. They take no notice of the occasional passing car or a late or early pedestrian.

They are talking. They may be arguing. He puts an arm round her shoulders, she opens the passenger door. He restrains her from getting out of the car, reaches across with his other arm and turns her head so that she faces him. He tries to kiss her, but only connects with her pale cheek. She pulls away but he is saying something in her ear, and she is listening. He succeeds in kissing her lips although she does not make it easy, her head remains upright and she looks along Pimlico Road. Now she sinks down in the passenger seat and inclines her head backwards, as if to offer him her lips. He kisses her, leans over, is dominant, shifts in his seat in order to be more on top of her, and the kisses seem to become passionate. She objects to something he has done, pushes him aside, rises up, possibly scolds him, opens her door again and struggles out. He is laughing at her and perhaps calling her back. She crosses the pavement, trips across in her long white dress, unlocks the door of a house, enters and closes it. He lights a cigarette, starts the car and drives off fast with loud exhaust noise.

PART ONE

She was Celia Farr, twenty-one years of age, a Christian, a virgin, and a trained nurse. The door she had unlocked was at the side of the antiques shop called Wellingham. She was staying the night with her friend Dot, Dorothy Wellingham, the daughter of Geoffrey Wellingham, proprietor of the shop, and his wife Sandy, who all lived over it. The name of the man in the sports car was Owen Pennant.

Celia was born and bred in Broadstairs, Kent. Her father was Bernard Farr, schoolmaster. Her mother, Christobel, known as Chrissy, worked in the little local Museum of the Sea, and as receptionist in a solicitors' office. Celia Farr's paternal grandfather lived at Westgate-on-Sea – Bill Farr had also been a schoolmaster. Her mother's mother was a widow ekeing out her existence in sheltered accommodation in Ramsgate. The Farrs were Isle of Thanet people. Celia's home was 42 Thanet Steps, a semi-detached Edwardian three-bedroomed seaside house in a back street.

She was an only child. She was the type of child who stares – her eyes were big and dark blue, her gaze unwavering and possibly critical. She was good, polite, bright and quite affectionate; also independent and strong-willed. She was at once fairy-like and tough.

Her father adored her, her mother was jealous, she was fonder of her father – they were a predictable family in some respects. Bernard Farr taught English at The Welcome School, and was Deputy to the Headmaster, William Hauntly, known as The Ghost. He had been employed by Welcome pre-war; had served in the army while the School was closed; and been able to buy ten per cent of the relaunched establishment after peace broke out. He was a cheery, sporty, unsentimental good chap, and treated Celia like a son. When his wife Chrissy moaned that she was unfulfilled and underestimated, he would take Celia to the park to kick a football about or play cricket. He was a slow left-arm bowler and would put up a stump and tell her to keep wicket. In the evenings, when she was in bed, he would give her a hug and a squeeze, which made her laugh: as a result her mother would say, 'That's enough,' and switch the light off and on resentfully.

Celia was taught her ABC by her father, then attended the Lower Class at Welcome. She did not flourish there. Co-education startled her, she was shy of boys, and embarrassed to be the daughter of the Deputy Headmaster. But when she was eight she moved into the Middle Class and met and made two friends, Constance Shelby and Dorothy Wellingham. Con was plump and giggly, Dot was a bean-pole. Con was bad at her books, Dot was clever. Con's father worked in a bank in the City of London, Dot's had recently moved his antique business up to town:

the former was of special interest to the girls because he left Broadstairs at five on weekday mornings and only got home at eight in the evening, the latter was remarkable because he lived in London during the working week. Dot's mother was interesting for two different reasons: she had a boy's name, Sandy, and was inclined to call herself 'a grass widow'.

The three girls fell into friendship almost at first sight. They were close without ever being distant. They sat near one another in lessons, held pow-wows during breaks, walked round the playing field together if they were not involved in games, talked and laughed non-stop, and never fell out. Their conversational topics in order of importance were: their pets; hair styles; how babies are born; what was wrong with boys; their crushes on boys; school and holidays; their parents; and their physical developments and natural functions.

Celia and Dot ascended into Upper Class six months before Con: they had to relate to Con the full story told in Biology. They were all pretty disgusted by childbirth, but it had its exciting sides. Puberty likewise – they were proud of their new selves, and humiliated to discover they had a lot in common with chickens.

Forms of romanticism now preoccupied them. They read books about love and, with luck, sex. They bought and repetitively played records of light tenors singing soupy ballads. They discussed courtship, marriage, maternity, and their wedding dresses. They studied boys from a different angle, and wondered how on earth their mothers and father could have conceived them.

At the same time they all experienced difficulties at home. Celia turned against her guinea pigs, and was rebuked by her father for giving her mother – who claimed that she could not let them starve – an additional cause for complaint. She had outgrown her teddy bear, and, she protested constantly, her clothes. She was unwilling to play football and cricket with her daddy, and when she did deign to be wicket-keeper she would drop the ball and let the bowler run after it. She was funny about paternal embraces, and turned the back of her head for her mother to kiss. She was a 'changed girl', an 'ungrateful girl', and 'unfeeling' according to Chrissy Farr, and she brought tears into the eyes of Bernard on several occasions.

Dot was creating similar problems. Sandy Wellingham tried to enlist Celia's help in dealing with her daughter's moodiness and uncertain temper: Celia shrugged her shoulders and said Dot was a sweet person.

Mrs Shelby also approached Celia. Con's mother had four children, three sons, then the daughter. She said Con had become so lackadaisical and lazy that her brothers called her 'the pudding', which reduced the girl to tears. Con never had been a cryer, Mrs Shelby said, she had been a laugher, but now she could not see a joke. Her father, Mrs Shelby said, was threatening to catch a later train home in order to see less of Con, and if he carried out his threat he would only reach Broadstairs at nine and scarcely have time to eat his dinner before he was rushing back to London.

The three girls were inclined to blame their parents, who were 'stuffy ... out of date ... intolerable'. A symptom of their indispositions was an inability to reason why. They were disturbed secretively by their hormones, and, consciously, by the wall of difficulties that seemed to loom up between themselves and the future. They talked of jobs, of remunerative work: which was bad enough. But they were not fools or exclusively frivolous: the responsibilities of finding the men who would love them truly, of giving away their virginities, surviving weddings and honeymoons, and making babies and caring for them and being cared for by them, these tests and tasks that nature set were frighteningly oppressive.

They finished with schooling in their eighteenth years. None of them even thought of further education at a university: they were not academic, and in those days girls who were not brainy were not encouraged to waste their parents' money. Celia returned to Welcome as extra teacher to the children in the Lower Class, and helped to organise games. Dot assisted her father, serving on some days in the shop in Broadstairs and on other days travelling up to London to the other shop in Pimlico Road. Con landed a job at Chicque, the Broadstairs boutique, but soon lost it because she was too sleepy and overweight, and then had to settle for Boots.

Being grown up was a big change, and brought about bigger changes.

Celia realised that family and home shielded her from the pressures of the wider world, and almost forgave her mother. She was less impatient, and more willing to lend Chrissy a hand. She not only gave Chrissy advice in often hectoring terms, she sometimes asked for it.

In return, out of relief, and with gratitude, Chrissy Farr somehow resigned in favour of her daughter, and yielded to her youth and strength. In practice, she thanked her for favours instead of asking for them, and praised instead of criticising. One day she said: 'You're much prettier than I was, you've become very pretty, you know.' Celia had not known it. Celia was startled. She was stunned. Of course she had wondered if she would ever be pretty, but had hated her buckteeth, despaired of her freckles, prayed in vain to be taller, wished her two best friends would not study and metaphorically pull her face to pieces. As for her mother, her mother had previously been the sworn enemy of Celia's attractions. Praise from Chrissy had the extraordinary force of mercy. It was touching, exciting. It excited much more than her father's hackneyed compliments.

Celia thanked her mother and laughed as if in denial. Then she was persuaded that her mother was not far wrong. She again looked in the mirror and realised why she was whistled at by men and on the receiving end of pleasant and unpleasant attentions. Her reflection told her that her thick blonde hair moved nicely, her eyes were far apart, her nose was straight and small, and her teeth had reformed and were capable of a wide white smile. And she knew she was lithe and her body was slender and neat.

Her excitement was soon fraught with other emotions. She might be pretty, she was pretty, which was nice, but the consequences were leading to difficulties with the opposite sex. She was not a flirt; she was shyer than ever, more self-conscious, and felt hunted.

She was fearful for another reason. She was prettier than Dot and Con. If a man or men saw the three of them together, he or they looked at her. Dot was a handsome girl, but her nose was too long and she was gawky. Con was a sweet bundle, but not an obvious object of romance. The trio had always been a mutual admiration society: how long would that, could that, last?

She foresaw disruption of their triangular friendship. When they went to a movie in Broadstairs, and then ate chips from Frankie's barrow, she suffered from the idea that they were all under threat. She had to sit between them in cinemas in order to foil roving male hands. She linked arms with Dot or Con or both in the streets, so that she would not be pestered more than they were. When Con's father wanted to show her the workings of a great banking house, involving a day trip to London and lunch at a restaurant, Con did not like it and Dot was a bit put out although Celia had declined immediately.

She arrived at a possible solution of the problem,

or at least a postponement of what seemed to her inevitable, and in her forthright way broached the subject.

'I've been thinking,' she said.

The others expressed surprise, and there was laughter. They were in the attic playroom in Dot's home in Marine Drive, half-listening to her records. Celia sat on the floor, Con on the broken down sofa, and Dot on the rocking horse, her long legs dangling.

'I've got to break new ground,' Celia said.

What did she mean?

She was going to be twenty, she had hardly spent a single night away from Thanet Steps in her whole life, she was tired of being a mini-school-marm, the teachers at Welcome were either female, married men or her father, and she wanted to take a risk for a change.

'Oh dear,' Con said, and Dot asked: 'Is it sex you're after?'

They all giggled.

Celia said: 'Not only – not that – I want something different – and not stupefying.'

'Like what?'

'I don't know. I don't know yet.'

Con wailed: 'You'll go away!'

'Maybe.'

'And Dot may have to go to London!'

She was referring to Mr Wellingham's plan to shut up shop in Broadstairs and unify his two businesses in Pimlico Road and move his family along with his antiques.

'May or may not,' Dot said in her sharp way.

14

'Don't cry before you're hit, Con! You could keep me company in London, if the worst comes to the worst. Anyway, you've got three big brothers – you've got men to spare – and we can't marry one another, for heaven's sake.'

'I wish we could,' Con said, provoking more laughter, which was roughly the end of the conversation.

It was more like a beginning for Celia. The motives that had spurred her to mention her own wish were superseded by a rush of restlessness, she would clamber out of her rut as best she could and as soon as possible. She considered her options seriously. She had no particular talent; was not cut out to be a career girl; and was definitely not an adventuress. On the other hand she was supposed to be kind and believed she would be a loving mother. She remembered her deep relationship with her guinea pigs, Walter and Rose – Rose who turned out to be a boy – a relationship that only proved shallow when she forgot to feed them. She would like to make up for that lethal omission. She would like to compensate for the brief period of her mal-treatment of her parents. What she wanted was to do something better than she had done.

In the Lower Class at Welcome she was addressed as 'Nurse' by a toddler called Theobald. It was Theobald's mistake. But she answered to the name. Impulsively she thought that Theobald had hit the nail on the head.

She broke the news to her father while they walked home after a day's teaching.

15

'It's a hard life,' he said.

'I'd like that,' she replied.

'Have you any idea of the range of a nurse's duties, hours of work, pay and so on?'

'I'll find out.'

'How long ago did you take your decision?'

'Yesterday, but I won't change my mind.'

'You never do.'

'Is that a fault?'

'No, no. Oh well, I was bound to lose you in one way or another.'

'You won't lose me ever.'

'Thank you, dear. I've been lucky to have had such fun with you. And you'll make a lovely nurse.'

Chrissy Farr was not averse to the prospect of having her husband to herself again, and responded to Celia's prospects merely by saying: 'Rather you than me.'

The grandfather in Westgate-on-Sea, Bill Farr, known as GranFarr to Celia, called her 'Sister', and Edith, a great-aunt, also confined her reaction to a single word: 'Fancy!'

The grandmother in Ramsgate, a self-pitier like her daughter Chrissy, said Celia would be able to make her comfortable on her death bed.

Dot said, 'Congratulations,' and Celia sensed that Dot too thought the time was ripe for the friends to search for their separate destinies.

Con listed the inescapable horrors of a nurse's work: bed-pans, catheters, enemas, injections, operations, amputations, and so on.

Celia applied to St Mildred's Hospital in

Canterbury for information and guidance. She read pamphlets, got through interviews, swotted and passed exams and tests, was accepted for training, worked long hours, slept in a dormitory with other would-be nurses in a lodging from which men were strictly excluded, and did not complain. She was branded a crackpot for enjoying herself.

Her weekends off and holidays were spent at Broadstairs. The Wellinghams had removed to London, but Dot sometimes stayed for a night or two with the Farrs in Thanet Steps. She would sleep on cushions on the floor of Celia's bedroom, and occasionally Con would bring round an inflatable mattress and doss down too.

The friends' main topic of conversation was now boys, men, suitors or the lack of suitors. They were all twenty-one – slow off their marks even by the current sexual conventions. Dot was considering two proposals, one from a limp youth who painted furniture to make it look good enough for her father to sell, the other a customer, who actually bought the furniture painted by his rival – the latter was getting on for forty, divorced, father of two, but also rich and amorous. Dot was afraid the first might be impotent as well as poor – he only seemed to want to hold her hand – and that the second would be all too virile – she had so far fought tooth and nail to permit no more than manual liberties. Con, unexpectedly, had a follower who appeared to be faultless – twenty-six, well-to-do local family, handsome, gentlemanly and keen – whom she dared to call 'Serf' and teased with the yes-and-no routine. Celia confessed that she loved nobody 'in that way' – she had fended off all the medical students, doctors and importunate patients – and said she must be frigid.

They discussed the question of whether they could be or would be 'aroused'. They agreed they would like to have children, and were prepared to pay the price. They talked of almost nothing else. Celia regretted the fact that she had no time to read books. Dot said she was not sure she liked the thrills and spills of London. Con said she was being driven mad by her mother. They missed one another, they agreed.

They planned a reunion at Broadstairs on one of Celia's free weekends in the month of July. But Dot developed appendicitis and rang to ask Celia a favour: her father had taken tickets for a charity ball, she had been roped in but was now out of action, would the friend of her family come to the rescue? Mr Wellingham's party so far included himself and Sandy, his best customer and wife, and a single businessman. Celia demurred. Dot said she could spend the night in the Wellingham home, in her bedroom there, and wear the dress that Celia knew, had once tried on, and loved, the white one with spangles.

Celia obliged. She arrived at the Pimlico Road premises at seven o'clock by arrangement. She was overwrought and frightened – Dot was still in hospital. But Mr Wellingham greeted her gratefully, and Sandy was kind, led her up to

Dot's room, which had a bathroom adjoining, and left her to change.

She wallowed in a bath, then tested the perfumes and used some of the make-up on the dressing-table. She had never known such luxury. The dress fitted. It had an upstanding collar, a snugly shaped bodice, a long skirt glittering with the spangles, and seemed to weigh nothing. Her last look in the full-length mirror was satisfactory. Downstairs the Wellinghams were complimentary, and Mr Wellingham ushered her out and into a chauffeur-driven car. They arrived at a hotel in Park Lane, queued to enter a ballroom where a band played, were directed to one of the tables laid for dinner, and introductions ensued. Celia shook the warm large hand of a man of thirty or so – the businessman, Mr Pennant.

She was seated next to him. On her other side was a deaf old gentleman, no doubt the 'best customer'. She had scarcely taken her seat when she was asked or rather commanded to dance. Mr Pennant immediately danced so close that it flustered her – it was another first, she had never had such detailed practical experience of male physiology. He did not talk, and she was too breathless to try. He returned her to the table, interrogated her, told her not to bother with her deaf neighbour – 'Concentrate on me,' he said, smiling at last. He had a gap between his front teeth and brown curly hair on his forehead, like a bull.

'You're Celia,' he said, either stating a fact or asking a question. 'Celia what?'

'My surname's Farr,' she replied – but she did not know how to talk to him, he was difficult to talk to. He had a sun-tan and dark brown eyes.

'Celia Farr, that's not bad,' he commented, as if she had been a wine and he was tasting it. 'Do you know my name?'

'No.'

'I'm Owen Pennant. I'm Welsh. Where do you come from? From under a mushroom, judging by your appearance.'

'I was brought up in Broadstairs – that's in Kent.'

'I know where Broadstairs is.'

Champagne was served. She had sampled it once before and hated it; but now she took a gulp and spluttered and sneezed. When he laughed at her, she found the strength to ask him to explain his reference to a mushroom.

'Because you're a fairy or an elf, that's what you look like to me,' he said. 'What are you in real life?'

'I'm training to be a nurse.'

'A nurse! You're wasted on your patients.'

He paid her other compliments: they bewildered, dazzled her – or was it the champagne? He went too far too soon, calling her beautiful, appetising, untilled, using other suspect adjectives, and saying she was at least an improvement on Dorothy Wellingham. She did not like it but could not stop herself listening, blushing, grinning foolishly, and hoping she was not behaving badly by the Wellinghams' standards.

Food arrived. She ate it without knowing if it was animal or vegetable. She drank white wine, and danced with him again, and willingly, either to stop him talking and cross-questioning, or because he did dance well, or for another strange reason. Her father had never held her as she was held by Owen. Although she had slapped men at St Mildred's who tried to get as close, she could not do so in this ballroom, in front of all these smart people, and was not even inclined to.

He insisted on her calling him Owen. He called her 'Twinkle'. He pretended to dread midnight, when he expected her to hurry back to sit by the ashes of her home-fire and be abused by ugly sisters. He made her laugh. He pressurised her to encourage him. Dot and Con would have thought him 'cocky'. He was sure of himself, arrogant, spoilt, certainly rich, and not a good sort and quite possibly a bad lot – she knew it all, but her anatomy overrode her critical faculty and her common sense.

She ate meat and drank red wine, she ate a pudding and drank more champagne. She drank sips, she was not drunk, but something had gone to her head. She was trying to maintain her dignity, to preserve her individuality, to have reservations and remember rules, but their dances betrayed her secrets, she felt. Discretion was somehow beyond her when he was so indiscreet, so intrusive and seductive.

Sandy Wellingham told her that they were going home, likewise the other couple. Owen

Pennant said he would drop Celia back at Pimlico Road shortly.

Sandy asked: 'Do you want to stay? Don't do as Owen tells you. What would you like to do, Celia?'

She hesitated. There was laughter, and she missed her opportunity to say, 'Save me, take me with you!' She was being kissed good night by Sandy, given a key to the front door of their house, and getting instructions about burglar alarms from Mr Wellingham. The 'best customer' and his wife said goodbye. Celia overheard Sandy's aside to Owen, 'Take good care of her,' meaning herself; and then he and she were by themselves in the crowd.

She was torn in two by excitement and terror. They danced again – it was better than struggling to talk and worse in that it seemed to rob her of the vestiges of self-control. When they returned to their table he looked at his wristwatch and accused her of keeping him up too late.

'I'm a working man, I'm at my desk at seven-thirty,' he said. 'Come on, let's pack it in.'

She was quite furious with him. She was sure she worked harder than he did, and for less money. Yet when he took her hand and pulled her towards the exit she hung on and squeezed his.

At last they were in his car, in the dark, in the rush of fresh air. He did not speak, she could not – anyway, because the car was open and noisy, speech was impossible. Her heart thumped – would he hear it, she wondered. What was going to happen, she wondered. He pulled up outside the Wellingham shop.

'Thank you very much. Good night,' she said, fumbling with the door handle.

'Where are your manners?' he retorted.

'What?'

'Highwaymen used to say "Your money or your life!" '

'What do you mean?'

'A kiss or yours.'

'I don't ... I can't ...'

'Don't be stupid, darling.'

He put his arm round her shoulders. She succeeded in opening the door of the car. He reached across with his other arm and turned her face. He managed only to kiss her cheek. She pulled away, but did not get out of the car. He was speaking, whispering into her ear, saying amazing things.

'Relax – let go – you'll learn a lot from me – we may be dead tomorrow – I can give you thrills you've never dreamed of.'

He was kissing her tightly closed lips. She was aware of tears in her eyes. She could not move or escape. She sank down in her seat and turned her face in his direction. She shut her eyes and realised she was crying or panting.

Celia spent the rest of that night or early morning alone, but did not sleep. For breakfast she had a cup of coffee with Sandy – Mr Wellingham was already moving furniture in his shop.

'I didn't hear you return,' Sandy remarked.

Celia understood the question, and replied: 'I tiptoed – we didn't stay much longer at the ball – I must have been back here soon after you were.' And she thanked her for everything.

'Did you enjoy yourself?'

'Oh yes.'

'You had a success with Owen.'

When Celia blushed, Sandy added: 'I can see he had a success with you.'

She continued: 'What did you think of him?'

'I didn't have much time to think.'

'No – he's quick on the draw.'

They laughed, and Celia began: 'Sandy' – she and Con had been told to call Mrs Wellingham by her first name, but still addressed Mr Wellingham formally – 'he's not married, is he?'

'Never – not quite, he's been hooked by a good few women, but not landed.'

'What's he like – really?'

'Very clever at making money, and thinks he can buy anything. No, that's not fair. Sorry, my dear. He's a charming Don Juan, but he isn't nasty to women and might be domesticated. Did he mention another meeting?'

'No.'

'Hard lines! They seldom do. May I state the obvious?'

'Please.'

'Don't give him everything he wants for nothing in return.'

'Oh but he couldn't be interested in me.'

'Why not? Don't underestimate the worth of

24

your wares. You see, I'm not my mercantile Geoffrey's wife for nothing. You'd better hope Owen values you as highly as you deserve. If he doesn't, more fool he!'

'Thank you, Sandy.'

Celia returned to Broadstairs and spent the second and last night of her free weekend in Thanet Steps.

Her parents noticed a difference in her. Her mother thought she looked well, perhaps suspiciously so, her father thought she looked tired.

Bernard Farr said: 'You'll find us awfully bread-and-butter, dear, after the jam of that swish house of the Wellinghams and waltzing the night away in Park Lane.'

'Oh Daddy!' she scolded him. 'Of course I won't. And I wasn't waltzing, we don't do waltzing any more.'

'Is that so?'

Chrissy Farr asked: 'Did you get off with someone, Celia?'

'No, Mummy.'

'Did Geoffrey Wellingham dance with you?'

'No, he didn't, but he and Sandy were tremendously nice.'

'Who did you dance with?'

'I can't remember – it was a big party – I never knew anybody's name.'

'But you had lots of dances?'

'Not lots – some – we had dinner to eat – and we weren't very late – we were back in Pimlico Road at about one o'clock.'

'I see.'

During the weekend Celia went for a walk with Con, who was thankfully more interested in her own love-life than anyone else's. Con satisfied her curiosity about the charity ball with a brief question and answer routine, and was in a hurry to report that she had actually slept with the 'serf'. He was a land agent, which was apparently much better than being an estate agent. He was called Ian, Ian Thornton – 'a pretty dull name, but it suits him,' Con said. She and Ian had been together at local dos – he was an amateur actor and played 'older' parts – 'the gravedigger in *Hamlet*, for instance,' she giggled. 'Poor old Ian,' she remarked apologetically, 'I mustn't make fun of him.' Anyway, while Mr and Mrs Shelby were on holiday, Con had their home in Kentish Road to herself. She invited Ian to supper, there had been a spot of canoodling afterwards, and then his car would not start, a development that would have been promising if Ian had not called in the AA, who towed the car away. She said to him, 'Stay the night,' and he said to her, 'Thank you' – not exactly romantic. They adjourned to her bedroom – she had not dared to let him sleep between clean sheets. They undressed in the dark, but she kept her underwear on and stipulated that he was to wear his boxer shorts. Her bed was so narrow that they were a sandwich almost from the word go. The rest was all anti-climax. He shook with nerves, she had had a heavy day stocktaking at Boots, and after false starts and commiserations she fell asleep.

In fact they both slept like logs. At least they agreed in the morning to have another bash at it, and no damage was done.

Celia laughed at the story, then asked: 'When is the next bash taking place?'

'I haven't a clue. Poor Ian – he moves more mysteriously than God.'

'But do you love him?'

'I do. Of course I do. There's no other man around.'

'Are you planning to marry him?'

'Well – seeing's believing, isn't it? I'm waiting to see.'

Celia wished Con luck, and in the afternoon of the same day fitted in a visit to Dot in a nursing home in the Harley Street area.

Dot also had a story to tell without delay. Her surgeon, Mr Pinner, was dark and dreamily handsome and had wonderful warm hands. Shaking hands with him was almost too much for her, and when he palpated her naked stomach she thought she would disgrace herself somehow. She was now counting the minutes until he came to take her stitches out.

Celia laughed with Dot, and they both laughed at Con's damp squib, then Dot asked about the ball.

'Who was meant to have been my partner?'

'Owen Pennant.'

'Was he one of Daddy's frightful old customers?'

'No.'

'Did you have a ghastly time? Those charity balls are such a sweat.'

'It wasn't like that, he wasn't like that.'

'Mum said you looked a dream in my dress.'

'Thank you for letting me wear it. Your room was lovely and your people were lovely to me.'

'No, don't mench – it was angelic of you to give up half your weekend, when you might have been with your parents.'

'I enjoyed myself. Honestly! I'd never been to such a grand party.'

'Oh well – I'm glad.'

They reverted to the subject of Mr Pinner, then Celia said goodbye.

Travelling back to Canterbury and St Mildred's, she mentally measured the chasm that had opened between herself and her parents and friends. Perhaps the chasm was an abyss, into which she had fallen and suffered damage to body and soul. She was no longer the person they had known. She herself no longer knew the person she had become, who told lies and sanctioned misunderstandings. Nobody else's love stories bore the slightest resemblance to the tongues of flame leaping inside her.

She tried to dowse them down. She poured cold water on them. But they were inextinguishable. They flared again and again. They were acquiring more intensity. But it was all as ridiculous as Dot's and Con's games with men. A few hours in Owen's company could not make so much difference. He could not have changed her from one girl into another overnight. Where was her strong character? What about her nurse's training, and her adoption of scientific approaches to life and death?

Romance should bear no resemblance to what had happened at the charity ball and in that rightly named sports car. She had expected romance to be like friendship that slowly expanded into love, marriage, sex and motherhood. She had thought it would be beautiful, not brutal, not bestial. She had been waiting to give her consent, not to be bullied.

She tried to despise or to pity Owen Pennant. He was a playboy. He wished to kiss or be kissed good night. The scene in his car, under the stars, could be regarded as a variation of 'Night night, sleep tight'. But she had not slept. She could not sleep in her babyish bedroom in Thanet Steps. She had seemed to cease to need sleep. She pined for the taste of his mouth. She was homesick for his embrace. She balanced on the tightrope of joy, with no net below, and misery underneath.

She was back at work at St Mildred's. A matron called her absent-minded: 'What's wrong with you, Celia?' She was shamed into pulling herself together – she had been proud of her reputation for dependability. Nothing worthwhile would happen. Nothing much had happened, she told herself. In the past, long ago, she had tried dancing close to boys, and boys had tried it – but those were clumsy experiments, minus the x-factor. She had been kissed by boys – meaningless kisses that involved her in nothing. One of the doctors had cornered her in the laundry, but the consequences were only a wrestling match and accusations that she was a lesbian. She suspected

Owen would categorise their dances and kisses as trials similar to hers, amusements, and a way of making the best of a bad job at the charity ball. 'Twinkle' was not her real name. He would have difficulty in finding her, and more in contacting her at the hospital. He had not bothered to ask any of the important questions. She must not waste her whole life in hoping to hear from and see him again.

Yet she had attracted him. She was aware that the attraction was mutual on the dance floor. On the other hand somebody had said – or she had read – that men were not like women inasmuch as they were not choosy. Owen's physical compliments might have been routine, a mechanical reaction to the proximity of female flesh. But the last of his kisses must have meant something to him since it meant everything to her.

The empty days passed. She fell from the tightrope and clung by her fingertips to the net. Misery was her next stop – if there was to be any stopping. She had chances to read when she did night duty; 'events' – hospital jargon for mortal crises – were minimal. She chose the saddest stories and shed tears over *Tess of the d'Urbervilles.* She envisaged spinsterhood – she would be the sort of spinster faithfully grieving for the man who was loved and lost. She belaboured herself additionally for having missed opportunities. Why had she not begged to be taught, when he had said she had a lot to learn? Why had she not asked him to make love to her there and then, in public, and in spite of the gear lever?

Eventually she was almost accustomed to her sore places. In this period of new experiences, she had been faced with a test never bargained for, and had summoned the energy to scrape through it. She was blooded, initiated up to a point, and certainly bloody, but unbowed. Taking matters into her own hands, tracing and tracking Owen, was not done; and if it had been, if she had been living when it was done, she would have been too diffident to do it. She was not so arrogant to wish she could or should reverse the natural roles of the sexes. If Owen did not want her, so be it – he was probably right – and he might be protecting her in a roundabout way. She would not criticise him adversely. She was lucky to have spent one evening in his arms, roughly speaking. The refrain of the song of love was that there were as good fish in the sea as ever came out of it; which was supportive, even if she was convinced that it was inapplicable to her case.

She smiled by day, and reserved her tears for the night, for the privacy of beneath the covers of her bed in the dormitory of trainee nurses. She had taken happiness for granted. No – she had been childishly blithe, blinkered and blithe, self-centredly blithe – and then ecstatic – and then wretched. She had yet to know happiness. She could not imagine what happiness was like. But she did not sink under the waves of her unhappiness, and derived some satisfaction from being able to keep afloat.

A month or so after the charity ball she received a letter. She did not recognise the writing, the postmark was London. She tore it open; but it was from Sandy Wellingham.

She read: 'Dear Celia, Owen Pennant would like to see you again. If you're interested, drop me a line to say where he could reach you. Oh yes, telephone number, too. Hope you're saving lives. Love, Sandy.'

She replied without delay. She listed the days on which she was doing night duty: she was free from four until eight on those days. She thanked Sandy with underlinings for writing.

Amazement mingled with doubt was her response to fortune's favour. That he should take trouble to try to see her was amazing. The rush of blood to her face, head, body and extremities while she read Sandy's letter was more so. That the long-drawn-out storm of her emotions subsided in a minute or two was almost miraculous. She could scarcely remember how wretched she had been. She looked forward to the future impatiently.

Of course she was dubious, too. How could they see each other – he was in London and she in Canterbury? How could a busy man find time to ring her, why would he, why should he?

He rang at five o'clock on the first of the days she had listed in her letter to Sandy. She was standing by the pay telephone in the corridor outside her dorm.

'Celia?' he queried.

'Yes.'

'This is Owen Pennant. Do you remember me?'

'Yes.'

'We were with the Wellinghams the other day.'

'Yes.'

'Where are you speaking from? Your voice echoes.'

'It's a public telephone.'

'Can you hear me?'

'Very well.'

'If I was ever near Canterbury, could we have a drink together?'

'I'd love to.'

'They seem to work you hard. What are these afternoons off?'

'I'm free before night duty.'

'Night duty? I wouldn't object to some of that. Is tomorrow any good to you?'

'What?'

'You're free at four, aren't you? What about four tomorrow?'

'Yes.'

'Do you mean you'll meet me at four o'clock outside the main entrance to the hospital tomorrow?'

'Yes – thank you very much.'

'I'll take you out to tea.'

He was laughing, laughing at her, laughing at himself, because tea in the country was not his line. She saw the joke and joined in. He rang off.

Her mood of semi-suspended animation carried her through the intervening hours. In the afternoon of the next day the sun shone – it was

33

August and a heat wave. She wore her usual civilian summer clothes, shirt, skirt and sandals – she had nothing smart in her locker.

He was standing by his car at a little distance. The car was sky-blue – she had not noticed its colour in the night. He wore an open-necked white shirt and red slacks. He did not see her at once, and his appearance, his pose, his clothes and car were like an advertisement or a scene in a film. He looked remarkable, powerful, out of the common run.

She approached him. He welcomed her – a smile, a move in her direction, no kiss – and opened the passenger door of his car. She slipped in, he got in the other side, and they were again sitting where they had sat. It had all been slightly awkward, but she did not mind that – instinct told her it was as it should be.

'What shall we do?' he asked. 'Do you really want to be taken out to tea like a schoolgirl?'

They again laughed in unison, she said no, she would be eating hospital food at seven, and he suggested Whitstable – 'Shall we have a look at Whitstable?'

They did not talk much during the noisy breezy drive. Then they found a spot of dry sand on the Whitstable beach and sat with their backs against a breakwater. The calm sea lapped in and out, and hurdy-gurdy music reached them faintly.

'Is it comfortable enough?' he asked.

'Yes. I'm used to sand and shingle.'

'I come from wild Wales,' he said, and picked up a pebble and tossed it aimlessly away.

'Have you been busy today?' she inquired in order to break a silence although she knew it was a boring question.

'I've driven to see you.'

'But I thought...'

'I don't do business in Canterbury. You're my business in Canterbury.'

She would have giggled if she had not been so tense.

She said: 'It's a long way from London.'

'I didn't think so, and I was right.'

He threw another pebble.

'Tell me what you do,' he said.

'I've been nursing for a year and a half.'

'Do you nurse men and women?'

'And children.'

'Are the men shy with you?'

'Not when they're ill.'

'Are you shy with them?'

'It's the same – you can't be shy when they're ill.'

'Are you shy with me?'

'You're not ill.'

He laughed.

'You'll get used to me,' he said. 'You will if you're patient – or have you other fish to fry?'

'What do you mean?'

'Have you got a boyfriend?'

'No – not a special one.'

'I'm not a boy – I'm thirty-one. How old are you?'

'Twenty-one.'

'I'm ten years older than you are, and I've

35

been around. That's one of the differences between us. I'm here partly because of the differences. Don't let me be a bother to you.'

'You're not. You couldn't be.'

'You're the stuff to freshen up a jaded palate.'

'What?'

'Nothing. You know nothing compared with all I know. I'm not being rude. Your ignorance is your point for me, my experience could be hell for you.'

'I'm not as ignorant as all that.'

'All what? Don't answer. I'll try again. You're not like the women I'm used to, which is more okay for me than for you. I'm not like the boys from Broadstairs or your invalids.'

'Who are your women?'

'Ghosts. I used to know young girls, but they didn't go in for useful work. I never was a monk, and I've been called fickle along with other names. Freedom has disadvantages. That's another reason to be in Whitstable.'

'I'm sorry, I'm not sure I understand.'

'Forget it – my method of clarifying issues with the opposite sex can lead to more misunderstandings. Have you any idea of my business?'

'No.'

'I'm a chartered accountant.'

'I know what that is – there's one at St Mildred's, and my father had a friend who's an accountant.'

'They wouldn't be anything like me. I'm Croesus. My work is to earn parts of businesses by improving their business. I look at the books

36

of firms, tell the owners how to do better, and in return they give me a share of the equity. Are you with me?'

'Sort of.'

'I make money as a result.'

'I see.'

'Women usually can't read the bottom line.'

'Mr Simms only helps my father with his tax.'

'Mr Simms wouldn't be a rich man.'

'No, he isn't.'

'I follow in my pa's footsteps. He made money in haulage when he was young, and then bought and sold land in Wales. He gentrified our family. I was reared like a princeling. Are you with me?'

'Yes, but ... I wonder – are you an only child?'

'Why ask?'

'Because I'm one.'

'The answer's no, not to speak of, I've a sister but I might as well not have one – Ruth, older than me and married to a Scotsman. We don't see each other, and the same applies to my pa. I've got beyond them, I've left them behind. Who cares? I don't! What's your family?'

Owen threw another pebble, which discouraged Celia.

'My father's a schoolmaster,' she said. 'He teaches at The Welcome School in Broadstairs.'

'News to me.'

'It's quite famous actually. I was a pupil there, and I taught there, too.'

'That's a claim to fame.'

She giggled and said: 'My father owns a bit of Welcome, but we're not rich or anything.'

'What's your mother like?'

'Not like me.'

'What are you like?'

'What?'

'You're ripe, you're ready for picking, you're a pupil now, not a teacher, I know that, but what goes on in your head?'

She blushed and hesitated. She was excited and outraged. She had been looking at the sea and straight ahead at nothing in particular throughout this conversation. Now she turned, was provoked to turn her head and look hard at Owen Pennant. He was smiling at her, as relaxed as a panther in a tree, so beautiful and luscious that her eyes filled with incomprehensible tears, tears of mingled love and hate, of desire and frustration and revulsion, and she burst out: 'You shouldn't ask me impossible questions, you shouldn't...' She failed to finish the sentence, she dared not scold him.

He laughed then and replied: 'You're right, I shouldn't. I shouldn't be here and shouldn't be standing you on that pretty head of yours. Take my advice, darling, give me a miss. I'm not a good boy, and you won't teach me different. There, I've said it. Let's have a drink before the credits roll!'

Abruptly he stood up, extended a hand, pulled her to her feet, and walked ahead of her in the direction of his car. She was horrified. Was he chucking her? Was he objecting to her half-hearted rebuke?

They walked to a pub. He had a gin and

tonic, smoked a cigarette, passed the time of day with the barman. She had a small sherry, could think of nothing to say to him, and began to wish she was dead. They did converse, but even more disjointedly, and by platitudes.

Soon he was saying it was time to drive her back to the hospital. She protested that she would be early. She could not believe that she had lost him and was lost.

They returned to his car. He drove off almost savagely. She was afraid she was going to cry. But he stopped in a side street with a screech of brakes.

'What's wrong?' she asked. 'What's the matter?' she besought him.

'This,' he said, switching off the engine and embracing her.

So the kissing began, and ended when he took hold of her left breast.

She pushed his hand away. It was involuntary, she was not ready, she might be acting against her interests, but she was unprepared and unwilling to submit to rough treatment.

He laughed at her and then drove on.

He said: 'That's something new – back to the class for beginners. Oh well, so it's got to be like riding a bike with no hands! You amuse me, you little primrose! You're a breath of fresh air. I'm guessing you're a virgin. You'd be fun for me, but I'd not be right for you – those are my last wise words, and could be my first, if it comes to that.'

She had to join in his laughter, even if it was at her own expense. She could not explain herself, she would not be able to find the words, or be tactful enough to convey her mixture of feelings. She let him mock her because mocking was preferable to goodbye. His kisses had been a great relief. They were expert kisses, thrilling kisses, but the best thing about them was that she was on the receiving end.

He dropped her at St Mildred's. He made one of his jokes by way of a goodbye: 'Steer clear of those big bad gynaecologists!' He did not mention another meeting.

Momentarily she was stricken by the omission. He was not planning to carry on with their affair – if it could be called an affair after her rejection and repudiation of his caress. At the same time, almost in the same moment, she remembered all the compliments he had paid her, verbally and orally, and was able to view the future in a not altogether gloomy light. Her intuition suggested that he might be back for more. She had plumbed at least the competitiveness of his nature.

Of course she had regrets, the curse laid upon lovers. She should have been quicker on the uptake, and not stumbled along in his wake. She had failed to entertain him, after he had driven so far. And how stupid she had been to resist him, considering she had rather loved his fondling, and, when all was said, wanted him wantonly.

But there was also opposition to such reasoning. On duty in the night, as she waited for a bell to ring or for her next tour through the wards, she recollected the difficulty of Owen, his un-cosiness, and that he was ten years older than she was and seemed to inhabit an alien planet.

She could not draw back. She could not politely even if she had wanted to. But her sweet captivity had connections with quailing. She drank cups of tea not only because night nurses did so in order not to fall asleep, and certainly not because she was sleepy: to the contrary, she drank them to steady her nerves and still an internal tremble.

Two questions nagged at her in the next few days. What would she say if he should either proposition or propose to her: secondly, what would she do if he did not?

She had her optimistic moments. She had proofs that for him she was an object of desire. And she was unfinished business after all, which he would probably want to wrap up in bed or elsewhere. Her farthest flight of fancy was to imagine that she was his destiny, as she was his.

But pessimism ruled. She was nobody, she was nothing. He could not stoop to care tuppence for her. There were millions of girls prettier than she was eagerly waiting to devote their lives to the service of a man like Owen Pennant. He was above her station, above her in all respects, and she was presumptuous to dream that he could ever be hers.

Despair drove her to seek consolation from Dot and Con. She still guarded her privacy, she could not bear to drag Owen's name into the dust of gossip. She rang Dot from the public telephone and announced that Mr Right was treating her wrong, and she was feeling mis. Dot replied, 'Join the club,' and went on to say that her surgeon had rebuked her for declaring that she was falling in love with him as he undid her stitches. Celia fared even worse with Con, who responded to her confession with the news that she was bitterly regretting having 'gone the whole hog' with Ian Thornton, who had turned out to be an absolute sex-fiend.

Again, as before, she tried to fill the vacuum with work, volunteered for extra duties, exhausted herself, and was more attentive to her parents.

He rang when she had ceased to expect to hear from him. He rang when she happened to be within earshot of the telephone. It was four o'clock on a weekday afternoon. She lifted the receiver in passing and stated the telephone number.

He said: 'It's Owen.'

'You...' she gasped, she repeated, and then, unstoppably: 'How wonderful!'

'I've been abroad,' he said, perhaps to apologise for not having rung sooner. 'I forgot to find out when you're reachable. Can you speak now?'

'Yes.'

'Are you okay?'

'Yes. Are you?'

'I want to see you.'

'Do you really?'

'When is your next free weekend? Come and stay with me in London.'

'Oh ... oh, heavens!'

'Are you putting off the evil hour?'

42

'I'm not – no – I'm free next weekend – it's Wednesday – I'll be free on Friday evening – but I've promised my parents...'

She lost her voice or her thread, and he laughed and suggested: 'You promised them not to stay with strange men in London?'

'No, no...' she joined in the laughter. 'I've promised to spend the weekend with them.' She was unaccustomed to fibbing and brought it out in a rush.

He saw through her.

'You're a good girl but a bad liar.' He was mocking her again. 'You'll be at Broadstairs, true or false?'

'Yes...'

'Will you allow me to be at Broadstairs?'

'What?'

'I'll come to Broadstairs.'

'Oh, Owen!'

'It's 42 Thanet Steps, isn't it? I'll call for you at eleven o'clock on Saturday morning – okay? What's that noise?'

'There are other people waiting for the telephone.'

'Did you hear what I said about Saturday?'

'Yes.'

'Does it suit?'

'Yes ... thank you! Thank you so much, Owen.'

She was thrilled for obvious reasons, and appalled by the prospect of having to introduce her parents to Owen and show him her home. They were dim and dowdy, and his car with the foreign name put her father's battered old Austin to shame. What would her mother say? What would her mother not say?

Eventually, at last, she arrived home in time for supper on the Friday evening. Her parents said she looked well, which was odd considering she had scarcely eaten for days and was worried stiff. Halfway through the meal, before the cheese and fruit, she spoke her piece.

'I'm going out with somebody tomorrow. He's calling for me in the morning.'

Her father said regretfully, 'Oh well, that's nice for you, dear,' and her mother asked, 'Is he your boyfriend?'

'He's my friend, he isn't a boy. I met him with the Wellinghams, when I stood in for Dot at that party in London. He's called Owen Pennant.'

She bit her lip, she was annoyed with herself for not keeping the tenderness out of her pronunciation of Owen's name.

Bernard Farr began to ask, 'What's his line of work?' when Chrissy barged in: 'Are you serious about him, Celia?'

'Oh, Mother – I don't know – and wouldn't answer if I could.'

'How old is he?'

'Thirty-two.'

'Good gracious! Is he rich?'

'Yes ... I don't know, I don't care.'

'It's not clever not to care, Celia.'

She called out, 'Father!' – as if to save her from her mother's inquisition.

'It's all right, dear,' he assured her. 'Any friend

of yours will be our friend. He'll get a warm welcome here.'

She shone a grateful smile at him, but felt she had to say to her mother: 'You will be polite to Owen, won't you?'

Her mother replied: 'I don't need to be told how to behave.'

The evening drew to an end, the night finally yielded to morning, and Celia's mix of emotions almost amounted to illness.

His car's powerful engine noise, an exception to the rules of Thanet Steps, announced his arrival. She opened the front door and stood in the doorway, waving both her hands at him defiantly. The weather was grey and damp, the soft top of the car was in place, and Owen emerged in checked golfing trousers, a red cardigan and open-necked pale blue shirt. He was extracting a great bouquet of flowers from the boot of the car.

Her embarrassment became reproachful. What would the neighbours make of his flashy clothes? Had the neighbours seen the flowers? He was compromising her, which was different from her compromising herself.

He carried the flowers in his right hand, and reached out his left by way of greeting her. He was smiling and saying, 'They're for your mother.' She took his hand and led him indoors, bewildered by events but impressed by his left-handed handshake. In the sitting-room, where her parents stood in front of the fireplace, he took charge of the introductions and presented the flowers.

45

Chrissy Farr's frown was replaced by a skittish smile and an offer of refreshment. Bernard Farr was asking for details of the drive down from London, and soon they were all sitting and drinking coffee together. Celia was silent. She was ashamed of her mother and even critical of her father's slow pronouncements. She silently loved Owen for being vivid and vibrant and a social star.

At half past eleven they left Thanet Steps. There had been badinage between Owen and Chrissy – 'I'm stealing your daughter away' – 'Bring her back in one piece' – and then they were in his car, they were pulled into the verge on a country road, in each other's arms and kissing.

That day was full of kisses. Their talk some-times seemed like background music. But everything he said was also like treasure to be gloated over at a later date. They walked in Deal, had lunch in a restaurant in Dover, bought return tickets for a cross-channel trip to Calais on Sunday, spent time in the fun-fair at Margate, drank local apple cider and ate fish and chips in a cosy pub in Sandwich, and parted at Broadstairs at ten-thirty, as arranged with her parents.

She had assured him that she had never been so happy. He had assured her in various ways that she pleased him, although love was not mentioned. He said: 'I was bored when you twinkled at me... You're what my doctor would have prescribed.' He said she was almost as much

46

fun as making money. He compared her with amber amongst the pebbles on the beach of Broadstairs, and the best apple in the orchard of Kent. He said it amused him to play at being boys and girls again.

He spoke autobiographically.

'I was born by Caesarian section – spoilt at birth because it didn't hurt... Ma was great, but I scarcely knew her, she died in a car crash when I was five – I inherited her soft spot for fast cars, she was killed in her Bugatti, she drove it into a tree... I did my first deal when I was nine or ten. I sold chickens that had been raised on one of my pa's farms – investment was zilch for many happy returns.' He referred to his 'flat' in London that sounded more like a house, it had an office with secretaries, and a staff of two, a married couple, cook-housekeeper and butler-odd-job-man, as well as his own accommodation. He revealed that he also had a house in Hertfordshire, called Pennygate. Moreover, even as he patronised and mocked her, he acknowledged her superiority in some areas. He asked for guidance in roundabout ways. For example he challenged her: 'How can you believe in God? ... What's so special about God? ... What's this faith that people bang on about?' He said: 'You think you do a better job than mine, you save poor people, I'm out to prove I'm rich – no contest, probably.' He asked: 'Money means independence – you and your family aren't really independent – why don't you worry?' He asked intimate questions, too. 'Why do you contradict

47

your kisses? They give me one message, you give me another – what's your game? Why not carry on from where your kisses stop?'

Towards the end of their day in the Isle of Thanet, his more personal questions were backed up by the urges of her own constitution. Chastity seemed hypocritical. She longed to say: 'Go ahead, now, now!' But she could not make the first move in that direction – it would have gone against her ladylike grain, against nature, against the form of their relationship. He was staying the night in a hotel near the golf courses in Sandwich: she wished she had shown interest in his room there.

He was boastful yet dissatisfied with himself and his life. 'I've got the lot, but it ain't enough . . . What's next on the agenda?' He was restless and knew it – 'I never got high marks for concentration. I should stop running around, but I get itchy when I'm not running.' Of all the perturbing things he said to Celia, at least perturbingly self-centred, the worst was: 'Gambling and girls are my scene – not a rosy prospect for a wife and mother.'

His personality was strong to the point of oppressiveness. He was beyond her, maybe above her, and distant when he was not close. He was comparable to a tiger in the zoo – he had to be approached with care. Metaphorically, he did to her those things described in cheap tales of romance, swept her off her feet, bowled her over. If he had not been glamorous, and not had a 'different' side, she would have fled and given him a general

48

thumbs-down. But he kissed so well, and they were on nearly equal terms while lips and their lives were in contact. She realised then, if briefly, temporarily, that she was invested by his desire with a kind of transcendent power. It was all new to her – all news. They kissed some more before she got out of his car at Thanet Steps, and she could not help agreeing inwardly with his parting shot: 'What about giving love a chance? Think it over! We could make beautiful music.'

On the Sunday, in Calais, there was no mistaking their happiness.

During the return journey, on the ship, she fell asleep with her head on his shoulder. She woke, looked at him, smiled, and he asked, smiling back: 'Do you love me?'

Her expression was affirmative as she asked: 'Could you? Do you?'

He embraced her, they embraced.

Then in his car, driving her from Dover to St Mildred's Hospital in Canterbury, he said: 'You wicked witch, I must see you again soon.'

She laughed, she was very flattered, and offered him her Wednesday afternoon off.

'Hopeless girl, it's not what I wanted, but it'll have to do,' he replied, and continued: 'Don't you yet know I'm impulsive? Wake up, sweetheart! You can't dangle a man like me on a string, and I won't be twisted round your little finger. So you can't accuse me of bullying, I'd just like you to pencil me in as a possible spouse. No comment – no commitment on either side – no publicity – there you are, a card on the table!'

He drew up at St Mildred's, would not let her speak, almost pushed her out of the car, and called out as he drove away: 'See you on Wednesday!'

She was in a dream for the next thirty-six hours, until the Tuesday morning, when she was rung by her mother early.

Chrissy Farr said: 'Owen Pennant came to see us yesterday evening.'

Celia was startled.

'He wanted our blessing. Can you hear me, dear?'

'Yes.'

'He's a fine man. We think you couldn't do better. Your father agrees with me. Owen's invited us to stay at his place in the country.'

'I must go, mother.'

'Don't be obstinate, Celia.'

'We'll talk another time.'

Celia was not pleased. At first she blamed her mother more than she blamed Owen. She realised that her mother had been brainwashed by materialism, Owen's flowers, signs of wealth, sweet talk and invitation; and that now her secret would be common knowledge in Broadstairs, and that she was going to be under pressure from all and sundry. Her romance was soiled by market forces. But her second thoughts were that Owen had broken his word about publicity. She was too honest to conceal the fact from herself that he had gone behind her back to force the issue of his peculiar proposal and rush her to the altar. Her doubts recrudesced, her spirits drooped. She was unsure of him, had never understood him, had been attracted to him for wrong reasons, because he was strange, a stranger, out of her league, a law unto himself, and unpredictable if not untrustworthy. What was she to do? He might not let her escape, he would not allow her to get the better of him. Her happiness vanished like the mists of morning. She saw a present fraught with indecision and controversy, and a future overshadowed by filthy lucre and not to her taste.

She dreaded Wednesday; it arrived nonetheless, and again he was standing by his car in the sunshine, in his summer slacks and a suede jacket, exuding manliness and confidence.

He drove her away from St Mildred's, from the humdrum world of difficulties and threats, into his almost imaginary kingdom of excitement, pleasure, novelty and hope.

'I called on your parents last Monday,' he said.

'I know,' she replied.

'They gave me the green light.'

'Yes.'

'I didn't want to be accused of baby-snatching.'

'I'm not a baby,' she said.

'And I'm waiting for you to prove it.'

They both laughed. Owen was funny. Everything was fun, after all. Their Wednesday hours together seemed to clarify their 'understanding'.

However, late in the evening, after dinner, human nature asserted itself, not only in physical communion but also in relation to seeing more of each other, and claiming more than they already had. He begged her to be a little more available, and she revealed that she could apply to take the week's holiday that was owing to her. He urged her to do so without delay. Amorous reasons apart, he wanted her to see Pennygate, and his flat in Belgravia.

Celia duly applied to the St Mildred's authorities, and was surprised to be granted leave of absence from that coming weekend until the next. She communicated the news to Owen, who said she must bring her parents to stay the weekend at Pennygate – he would send a car to Broadstairs, it would be at Thanet Steps at eleven o'clock on the Saturday morning. Celia was taken aback: she had thought he wanted to see her; she had not expected her parents to be included in this visit to Pennygate; she felt he was paying more attention to her parents than to herself; and who would be driving this car that was going to pick them up like parcels?

'I'm looking forward to seeing you,' he said.

'Oh yes – so am I – and thanks,' she replied.

Later in that day Celia happened to hear the public telephone ringing and ran to answer it. She was hoping that Owen might have decided to change the plan. But it was Con on the line.

'When's the wedding?' she began. 'Can I be your bridesmaid?'

Celia asked how she had heard such gossip.

'Your ma. Hasn't he been to ask your pa for your hand in marriage?'

'Oh Con! You know my mother too well to believe a word she says.'

'The rumour is he's a millionaire and drives a Mercedes-Benz.'

'I don't know what sort of car he drives. Who told you that?'

'My Ian saw you in an open Mercedes with a sun-tanned man. What's the true story?'

'I'm friends with someone called Owen Pennant. Okay, yes, I'm walking out with him. But I'm not marrying him yet.'

'What's he like? Is he really rolling in it?'

'He's nice. I'm not interested in how rich he is or isn't.'

'Golly, you're a heroine, Celia, not to mind about money. My Ian thinks of almost nothing but. It's money or sex with him, and I suppose it's beginning to be ditto with me.'

'Is he still pressing his suit?'

'Is he not!'

'Successfully?'

'Up to a point – no pun intended.'

'Are you going to marry Ian?'

'Maybe – he'd be better than Boots, provided he could afford me. I wish we could have a double wedding. If you were with me I could face it.'

'I couldn't be with you on the honeymoon.'

'Poor old Ian, he is a bit of a nagger. He's on and on about marriage. He's nagged me for saying the other day that if I let him have enough of me now, we might have got through the seamy side before the honeymoon.'

Yet another telephone call figured in this period of Celia's relations with Owen. She rang Dot

Wellingham to ask if she could stay at Pimlico Road for a night or two of her free week.

Of course, Dot said. She had been longing to see and talk to Celia. She knew about Owen Pennant, who had just invited herself, her parents and Celia to dine with him in his flat on the Friday evening of her holiday. Con had also dropped a hint or two. What was the state of play?

Celia confessed guardedly, and asked questions instead of answering them as soon as she could. Was the surgeon any good?

'Good at sending in a colossal bill, good for nothing else.'

'Oh well! London's full of men, Dot.'

'My new beau's one of Daddy's customers. He's a collector, he collects corkscrews and fire-irons and Chinese pots, and wants me to belong in his collection.'

'Are you willing?'

'No – able but unwilling – he's fifty and fat. Hope springs eternal. Look at what's happened to you!'

'Don't! Nothing's signed or sealed. I'm dithering intactly. You'll have to hold my hand.'

They laughed together, as Celia had laughed with Con. But life had become less light-hearted for her than it was before Owen introduced other people into the act.

The car that arrived on Saturday morning was a large black saloon. The driver was a middle-aged man in a blue suit, who called himself Ernest and Mr Pennant's 'factotum'. In the course of the drive Celia asked Ernest what sort of car it was and was informed: 'Mercedes-Benz, Miss.'

It embarrassed her that Owen should have a factotum, whatever a factotum was. She was embarrassed by Owen having two Mercedes-Benz, each of which must have cost many times more than the Farrs' Austin. That her father seemed to be bemused by Owen's lordliness embarrassed her, as did her mother's relentless matchmaking. Celia had not known she was swapping kisses with a millionaire. She had loved Owen for being well-dressed, for having the wherewithal, but had not done any sums. Now she thought of Pennygate as Poundgate, and felt like Cinderella with a difference, half-wishing she was not bound for his palace.

It was a house, and apparently not too big. She was pleased to see Owen again, and grateful to him for making a fuss of her parents. He showed them up to their bedrooms, Ernest following with the luggage. The Farrs had been allotted a large bedroom with a double bed and dressing-room adjoining, another single bedroom and a bathroom: all in a line, opening into a passage which was a cul-de-sac with a door at the other end.

Owen managed to murmur in asides to Celia: 'You see I'm playing your game,' and again, 'Note how difficult I've made it for myself,' references to her chastity. She was not responsive, she was afraid he would be overheard.

Lunch was three courses. Owen discoursed on the subject of Pennygate and its late owner, his Aunt Susan, his mother's sister, who had bequeathed it to him. In the afternoon he conducted a tour of the garden, and Celia noticed a wing stretching out at the back of the house, making it more roomy than its front suggested. He then drove them in the Mercedes saloon to look at his model farm.

Tea was served in the drawing-room, where lengths of a tree-trunk smouldered on a pile of ash in the grandiose fireplace. When Owen offered to show Bernard Farr his study-cum-office, Chrissy dragged Celia upstairs ostensibly to rest and change for dinner, in fact to listen to a lecture on the advantages of Owen as gentleman, husband, son-in-law, father, breadwinner and all-round attraction.

Dinner was too much of everything, and the period between dinner and bed-time was a strain. Chrissy was encouraged by Owen's wines to try to flirt with him. Bernard Farr cleared his throat continually, Celia's toes curled, the small talk ran out and Owen smoked cigarettes, looking pained. They retired to bed early thanks to Celia's announcement that she was dead-tired.

Sunday was again testing. Owen wanted Celia to meet some of his neighbours: that was how he put it. He had asked people in to drinks before lunch, more people to lunch, and still more to dinner. They were all older than Celia, and often older than Owen himself. They were mostly businessmen. There was a great deal of noise and chatter, which was better than awkward silences. Chrissy enjoyed it evidently, but Bernard was not used to social extravaganzas and cast despairing glances at his daughter, who was doing her best not to look as wet a blanket as she felt.

That evening, as the house party was on the stairs going up to bed, Owen told Celia that he had to go to Paris in the morning – something had turned up – he would be leaving early – and would she convey explanation and apologies to her parents?

'Has the weekend been all right?' he asked. 'I'll be back from Paris mid-week, and I've invited the three Wellinghams to have dinner with us on Friday night – they're good friends of yours, aren't they?'

She answered yes to both questions – she was dumbfounded, and seemed to have no chance to say more – she kissed him good night and he kissed her – and they went to their separate bedrooms.

In hers, as soon as she was alone, she was critical, rebellious and sad. He should have warned her about Paris before. He should have explained to her parents rather than ordering her to do so. He should have remembered that at his urging she had taken her week's holiday so as to be free. She suffered from a sense of loss: where was the Owen she had fallen for? She did not know what to do. She did not know what was going to happen.

On the Monday morning the Farrs were driven back to Broadstairs by Ernest in the Mercedes.

57

On the Tuesday and Wednesday they recuperated as if after shocks to their systems. On Thursday Celia was due to go to London; she was to report at Pimlico Road where the Wellinghams' shop closed at five o'clock and Dot would be free. After lunch on Thursday father and daughter walked along the Broadstairs beach, where they had played cricket once upon a time.

They harked back to days gone by, then Bernard said: 'You must have noticed that I haven't bothered you with words of wisdom and sage advice.'

'I have,' she replied, 'and I'm grateful.'

'Don't worry, I won't start now.'

'Thank you.'

'But...'

'Oh dear!'

'But, after much cogitation, I've decided I can't keep a secret from you. Owen spoke to me when he came to Thanet Steps on his own.'

'I know. Did you bless him?'

'No. But I didn't curse him either. Everything was hypothetical. Anyway, he spoke to me again at Pennygate. He gave me details of matters that might influence you, although I don't believe they will. He talked about a marriage settlement.'

'What's that?'

'Money that he would settle on you, give to you, if you were to marry him."

'How much?'

'Two hundred and fifty thousand pounds.'

'Well I never!'

'It doesn't stop there. He'd allow you a thousand

pounds a month, twelve thousand a year, pin money, for you to spend as you wish. You'd also have the interest on the quarter of a million.'

'Are you proud to have a daughter worth such a lot of lucre, Dad?'

'I felt faint when I realised how much you were or could be worth.'

'Good Daddy! I'm not bribable.'

'Good Celia!'

'Money makes a difference to me. It really does! It puts me off. It's causing me problems, Dad. I didn't have a nice time at Pennygate.'

'No – well – your mother and I were in the way, which didn't help. Owen hasn't done wrong to be rich. He's multiplied the money he inherited, and in the Bible a man like him was called a faithful servant. You'd find excellent uses for the money you'd have if you were Owen's wife, and it wouldn't necessarily be bad for your character. You wouldn't forget how difficult it is to make money, or how lucky you were not to have to worry about it.'

'Are you urging me to marry him, Dad?'

'No.'

'Are you telling me not to?'

'No.'

'What are you telling me?'

'You can choose either to be a nurse and wait for Mr Right, or you can choose to marry Owen.'

'Mother could make the choice without hesitation.'

'True.'

'A pity I've not got more of Mother in me.'

Later in the afternoon she hugged her father very tight on the up platform at Broadstairs Station.

His parting words were: 'I think you're a bargain at the price' – and they made her laugh.

Dot was the only Wellingham at home when Celia arrived – Mr Wellingham and Sandy were involved in some antiques fair. The two young women talked non-stop throughout the evening. Celia mentioned Owen intermittently, she could not stop herself speaking his name, but in response to Dot's initial questions she said she could not answer them, and would cry if she tried to. At other times she revealed that she was missing him, did not know him well enough, was bewildered in spite of their 'understanding', doubtful about his intentions, uncertain of her own, and was doing her level best not to go mad. For light relief they talked of Con and Ian Thornton, and Dot discussed her 'collector', Hubert Maclaghan, who was apparently refusing to take no for an answer.

On the Friday morning Mr Wellingham had business elsewhere and Dot was minding the shop. Sandy, sitting at the breakfast table with Celia, referred to Owen's dinner party.

'I can't imagine why he's asked us,' she said. 'We'll be playing gooseberry.'

She then noticed tears in Celia's eyes and asked: 'How's the romance going?'

Celia said she did not know, a phrase that was becoming her refrain, and added: 'He invited me and my parents to spend last Saturday and

Sunday at Pennygate, and asked lots of his friends in on the Sunday.'

'Did you enjoy that?'

'We didn't see much of each other.'

'Where is he now?'

'He went to Paris.'

'Wasn't this week your holiday, when you and he could make up for lost time?'

'He's invited you for this evening to please me, I think – and I am glad you're coming. He said he asked the people in at Pennygate for me to meet them, but they were his business cronies and wanted to meet him.'

'Dear me! Bachelors lead wild lives, they're wild animals, and we have to tame them.'

'Would he want me to do that?'

'It's the price he'll have to pay for you.'

'He's terribly rich. He's offered my father pots of money for me. I couldn't cope with the money side – we're not a financial family.'

'My dear Celia, believe me, you'd be surprised by how easy it is to cope with having more money than you've ever had before – what's difficult is vice versa, having less. Remember the witticism – money, not manners, maketh the man.'

'I wish – I don't even know what I wish – but perhaps I wish most of all that I was worthier.'

'Heavens alive! Owen's an outstanding man, but I'd never call him worthy. We've all been hoping that you were so good that he wouldn't dare to be unworthy.'

Later in the day Mr Wellingham returned and

took over in the shop. Dot was released to endeavour to calm Celia's nerves before the dinner party.

Owen's flat was in Eaton Square. The house was imposing, they were admitted by an entryphone, travelled up in a lift, were welcomed by a man in a white jacket, who ushered them into a sizeable hall and then into a large sitting room. It was brightly lit and seemed to glitter. Celia unexpectedly felt weak at the knees when she set eyes on her host.

She survived the sensation. She was a nurse and had watched operations in the hospital. She summoned her courage, and gradually the occasion caused her more pleasure than pain. Owen had not invited strangers to dinner. He sat her on his right at the dinner table and Sandy on his left – a breach of etiquette and a sort of honour. He kept on looking at her in such a way as to raise her temperature, and once, between courses, covertly held her hand. He included her in every conversation and sought her opinions. She was the centre of his attention, and recovered the confidence he had stolen in the earlier part of the week.

After dinner, when the ladies left Owen and Bill in the dining-room, Sandy said to Celia: 'He's yours, like it or not.'

It was the first of a trio of turning points.

The second was Owen's offer to fetch her from Pimlico Road on the next day, Saturday, and drive her back to Broadstairs.

The third occurred when she had gone to bed

in the spare bedroom of the Wellinghams' home. There, in the night, contrarily, it dawned on her that she was his at least as much as he was hers, and, by accident or design, by means of his expert male machinations or her innate subliminal female ones, she was trapped. Her alternatives actually were to marry him or to break her heart. She had gone too far while she thought she was going nowhere. She could not willingly retrace her steps, she therefore had to go farther, to the end of the matrimonial road. The best reasons were the simplest: she could not bear to lose him again.

She had one residual doubt and anxiety: would her unilateral decision telepathically inspire Owen to pop the question she was ready to answer in the affirmative?

Saturday was sunny, the hood of Owen's car was down, and they drove out of town and into the full summer leafiness of the country. In side roads they stopped for kisses, on main roads they shouted apologies, pardons and terms of endearment at each other. The rush of air as they sped along ruffled their hair, and Celia reached out her hand to smooth his down.

He knew a pub in the middle of nowhere. They parked nearby, at a wayside clearing in a wood, and got out of the car to embrace more comfortably, and he asked without preamble: 'What's the verdict?'

They were married in the church in Broadstairs where Celia had been christened and confirmed.

The wedding ring was engraved on its inner surface with the two words 'For Ever' – the engagement ring was a solitaire. The reception was held in the Shelbys' house – Con Thornton, née Shelby, had been one of the bridesmaids, and Dot Wellingham the other. The honeymoon was in Biarritz on the Atlantic coast of Southern France. The marriage was consummated within minutes of the couple finally finding themselves alone in their hotel bedroom.

They spent a fortnight in Biarritz. For Celia, it was a crash course in the realities of marital rites. Owen was virile, surely virile to an extraordinary degree, and she immediately derived satisfaction from their sexual exchanges. He congratulated her and himself on her responsiveness – she was a rare bird, he said; he also called her one of the quiet demure types who turn out to be sex-boxes in bed. His complete confidence as performer was infectious, and his expertise and ingenuity were aphrodisiacal. For both of them, but probably more so in her case, the novelty of commitment spurred them towards repetition.

Celia was happy. She had always been a cheerful girl, but now she was a happy woman. She was in love with Owen – he was the monarch of her heart and mind, body and soul, he was her pride, her destiny, and he reassured her over and over again that he reciprocated. His past was past, he was hers in the present. The faults she had found in him seemed to have been amended by his vows in church and the blessing of their union.

The sun shone on them in Biarritz. The weather was kind, and at night stars in a deep blue sky shone through the windows opening on to their balcony, and the breeze drifting in from the Atlantic Ocean was exceptionally balmy.

On the third or fourth day of their honeymoon she was aware of a change in Owen. He was again a little more like he had been and a little less like he had begun to be since marrying her. His attention wandered: it was no longer fixed on her good points, external and internal. His thoughts were elsewhere – their roads had diverged – there was distance between them – and she was disappointed, but not downcast. It was inevitable, she reflected. He was a professional man. He had his work at the money mill, just as her father had had his at The Welcome School. She forgave him for buying more newspapers and for being absent while he was with her. The knock-on change made itself felt in their sex life. Whether or not he noticed it, she had recourse to sex to reclaim him. The love that they made acquired another meaning, it was an axe to grind. She comforted herself by thinking her discovery was also womanly, and she was enlisting in the ranks of wives and mistresses through the ages, who had fought as she prepared to fight the battle of the sexes.

They travelled home. And the busy round of their life began. She had thought she might not have enough to do, she would become as lazy as she had been energetic before, especially at St Mildred's. She had made Dot and Con laugh by saying she would be surrounded by servants, hairdressers, manicurists and masseurs, while she lay on satin cushions. Not so: the opposite occurred. She was working overtime to win the friendship of Aunt Susan's old retainers at Pennygate and the staff in London and to remember their names; to house-keep two residences; to arrange, double-check, supervise, inspect everything, and not to be browbeaten by her staff; to dress well in order to be a credit to Owen; and to please or at least not to displease him.

At Pennygate there were Stanley the butler and Mrs Stanley the cook, Jean the housekeeper whose husband Bill was the head-gardener, two tweenies, who helped Mrs Stanley in the kitchen and Jean in the house – they were called Madge Bright and Dulcie Boon; and out of doors Ernest presided over the garage and cars, Bobby, a lad, was the under-gardener, and an old man, Mr Richard, did odd jobs. The Stanleys occupied one cottage, Jean and Bill another, and Madge and Dulcie occupied attic rooms in the house. Over at the farm, the manager was Arthur Otway, and he and his wife lived in the farmhouse. In London, in Eaton Square, the couple in charge were David the butler and Molly the cook – Mr and Mrs Arkwright. Celia formed friendships or alliances with all these people in a hurry. She could not have coped with Owen's way of life without their assistance, and she had to convince them that she posed no danger to their jobs.

The Pennants entertained in town and in the

country, and consequently were entertained. They had to go out in the evenings, stay for weekends, and agree to be included in shooting, fishing, golf and sailing parties. They were often weary, even exhausted; but Owen explained that he could not afford to be stand-offish and they had to repay hospitality. They were young, they recovered, and they had a good time, an interesting varied amusing time.

Celia was not going to complain of her lot and her luck, as some of the young women in her position whom she now met were inclined to. She was grateful to find she was somebody rather than nobody. She was glad to be pretty and popular, and to move in a circle where the arts and devices of womanhood were appreciated. She learned the lesson of how the world worked, ignorance of which is the commonest failing of women; and by means of discrimination she sought to improve the quality of Owen's guests and would-be hosts.

She had days off: a similarity with her previous experience. Owen would have to be somewhere else, she would be free to spend time with Dot, or to motor in her new car, a Mini, to Broadstairs to see her father and mother or Con. But Chrissy's triumphalist attitude to her daughter's marriage, Bernard's mournful queries, then her friends' efforts to be noticeably generous and her own not to be smug – all strengthened the magnetic charms of her life with Owen, its glitter and fun.

The months hurried by. A whole year passed

without Celia noticing that their intimacy had been partially eclipsed by their social engagements. One or the other or both were sleepy at night, and Owen had breakfast meetings in hotels. Weekends largely belonged to their guests or their hosts. It was natural, she reflected. The fires of desire had been bound to simmer down. Owen's work, or rather his ambition, was important and perhaps merited priority, she allowed. Her reflections, in so far as she had time to reflect on anything, brought home to her the fact that loving couples are designed by nature to replace the missing element with a baby.

Then it struck her that she had never started the suspicion of a pregnancy. Why not, for heaven's sake? It could not be for want of the necessary. She was a maternal woman, she now discovered she was pining to be a mother. She also wondered if she was failing Owen, she feared she might be, although he had not mentioned children. She felt healthy, had confidence in her constitution, had used no contraceptive devices – surely her prayers would be heard, she must be patient.

A postcard from her mother was cathartic. Chrissy had written on it, 'Where's my grandson?' She contacted a doctor she knew at St Mildred's, Dr Richard Leaf, a gynaecologist, and kept an appointment with him on one of her free afternoons. His diagnosis was that her Fallopian tubes were constricted, but could be cleared in a surgical operation that would enable her to conceive a child.

Celia returned to the flat in Eaton Square. She was longing to tell Owen that they could soon have a family. He returned late from a business meeting and wanted a quick bath – they were going out to dinner with friends of his. She waited for him in his dressing room. He emerged, drying himself with one of their huge towels.

'I've something exciting to tell,' she began.

'Go ahead,' he replied, casting the towel aside and opening drawers and cupboards.

'I've been to see a doctor.'

'Why? You're not ill.'

'It isn't that. I've found out why I haven't given you a baby.'

His head was in his clean white shirt.

'Sorry – what?'

'I need a little operation – on my Fallopian tubes – there are two of them and they're clogged up.'

'Spare me the details,' he said. 'I'm feeling sick already.'

'Aren't you pleased about a baby, Owen?'

'Female babies are better when they reach the age of consent.'

'But I was so happy for you,' she said.

He was tying his tie.

'I'm happy too, of course I am, but I'll have to leave the gynaecology to you. Are you dressed and ready?'

'Yes.'

'Well done! I'll be with you in a minute, and we can hit the road. Talk to the tall bald man tonight – he's called Thompson and I'm trying to get my hands on his crock of gold. Good news about the little one!'

As a result of this conversation Celia decided not to go ahead with the operation.

Their life was more of the same. The weeks and months continued to whirl by. Celia made umpteen acquaintances, but no friends. Men flirted with her, women were given no cause to be jealous, she was polite to everyone, and ready to hide her light so that Owen would shine the brighter. Their wealth was like a gauze in the theatre: they were on one side of it and the rest of the world was on the other, where outlines were softened and faces not quite recognisable. Celia had adjusted to a fate that bore resemblances to Cinderella's, but privately, following her decision to postpone the op, she was shocked to realise that her reaction to her prince had become objective.

She was not willing to have his child just yet. He was not ready. He was not a bad husband. He was not cross, violent, stingy, dull. He was still amorous sometimes, and never failed her if or when she was. But he was selfish. He liked to win, and was not interested in whom or what he had won. She was harmed by that characteristic, for he had begun to take her for granted, along with his money and houses and servants and social success.

Celia judged him as never before, but loved him still. She believed that one day, when she was more used to him and he was more appreciative of her, she would be able to have children and that they would fill the small area of vacuum in her marriage. Meanwhile she would 'soldier on' – one of her father's pet phrases.

She had been married for nearly two years, and a regular weekend party gathered at Pennygate.

It consisted of six guests: a married couple called Longden, stockbroker Mark and Tanya, a company director called Oliver with Lucy, his sleeping partner in every sense since she owned a large percentage of shares in his business, and another couple, Jim Town, a banker, with his American wife, Mary-Ann. Celia had feelings for two of the six: affection for Tanya Longden, and dislike of Mary-Ann Town. Mary-Ann was a career girl, raucous, provocative, striking rather than pretty, and too friendly with Owen.

Lunch on the Sunday in question was prolonged and noisy, and after it Tanya Longden agreed with Celia's suggestion of a siesta, Mary-Ann said she was ready to lie on her back, and they all drifted upstairs.

Celia had a snooze and prepared to return to the fray. On the landing at the top of the stairs she noticed that the door into the bachelor wing was ajar: which was strange as none of the bachelor rooms were occupied. A housemaid must have forgotten to close it. She went to do so, and heard a noise. She thought of summoning Owen, but instead tiptoed along the passage. The door of the room from which the noise issued was half-open. She pushed it and beheld Owen in a chair and Mary-Ann on her knees between his legs.

Mary-Ann raised her head, looked round at Celia, and said: 'Whoops!'

Owen was gazing at Celia in a recognisable way. He was also fumbling with his trousers.

Mary-Ann stood up and said to Celia, 'Sorry – but at least I've still got my knickers on,' and walked out of the room.

Owen now said, 'Celia,' in fairly plaintive accents.

She turned and ran to their bedroom and locked herself into the adjoining bathroom.

Owen followed her and said in a hushed voice through the door: 'Celia – Celia, let me in – please talk to me – we must talk – please!'

She stood, leaning back against the locked door, heard him out, then spoke in an equally quiet voice: 'Can you hear me?'

'Yes –'

'Listen! There's nothing to talk about. We've nothing more to talk about. Leave me alone, Owen.'

'No, I won't – please open this door.'

'Leave me, Owen. If you break down the door I'll jump out of the window.'

'Oh my God – be sensible – it was damn all – I drank too much – forgive me!'

'Goodbye.'

'What?'

'Goodbye.'

'Don't be silly! Celia! Celia, are you listening? You can't do this to me – I'm sorry – I'm grovelling – don't punish me too much for nothing. Where's your Christianity?'

He broke off, and a moment later said: 'The Towns are leaving, so's Oliver – I'll have to put in an appearance. My darling, think again! I can be tough – don't try to be tough on me – it won't work. I'll come and talk to you properly as soon as I can. I love you.'

He absented himself. She could hear the voices of the departing guests in the house and then out on the gravel sweep. She unlocked the bathroom door, seized a small travelling suitcase, stuffed underwear, shirts and a pair of jeans into it, snatched her bag which was luckily in the bedroom, retraced her steps along the passage of the bachelor wing, descended the staff staircase, and stole out of the house by a side-door close to where her Mini was parked. She drove to Berkhamstead railway station, left the locked car in the station car park, bought a single ticket to London, and caught the next London train which drew in a quarter of an hour later. At Paddington she found a telephone and rang her home in Thanet Steps.

Her mother answered and then spoke.

'How are you, Celia?'

'Fine!'

'And your gorgeous husband?'

'Fine!'

'Are we going to see the two of you soon?'

'Yes, Mother.'

'I know you're busy, but you should remember us, Celia. We were always good to you, and now it's your turn. Your father does miss you.'

'Is he about, Mother?'

'I thought you'd be wanting him. All right – here he is.'

Her father came on the line.

'Lovely to hear from you,' he said.

'Dad, I need to talk to you urgently and privately. Could you go to the phone box on the corner and ring me as quick as you can. I'm in another phone box and other people might try to get in.'

'What's your number?'

She gave it to him, blessing him for being so quick on the uptake, and waited for what seemed a century for the telephone to ring – no one had bothered her.

'Tell me,' he said.

'I've left Owen.'

'Are you safe?'

'Yes.'

'Where are you?'

'In London, near Paddington – I'm going to find a room with b and b.'

'Why, Celia?'

'He betrayed me. We're done for, it's all over.'

'Was it so bad?'

'Yes – for me, yes – I'll never go back.'

'Never say never.'

'I mean it.'

'Are you very sad?'

'Yes. But I swear that I won't kill myself. I'll be better one day. Dad, Owen will be looking for me. He'll ring you. Can you just tell him I'm okay, but have to be left alone?'

'If that's what you want.'

'I do.'

'Can I reach you, Celia?'

'I'll ring in a few days, when I'm organised.'

'I could come to London.'

'Thank you, Dad. Thanks for everything. You'd better go back to Mother – what did you say you were doing?'

'Seeing a man about a dog. You've got enough to worry about.'

Celia had one hundred and seventy pounds in cash in her bag: she had resolved not to use her cheque book on a joint account, and credit and debit cards were not yet available. She walked along Praed Street, into the Edgware Road, passed small hotels that charged too much for a single room, and in some poorer area farther north found a terrace of modest dwellings with advertisements for bed and breakfast in parlour windows. She rang a doorbell, but did not like the look of the man who opened the door, mumbled an excuse and hurried away. At the other end of the terrace she tried again. A respectable middle-aged woman opened the door. She had only one room to let, it cost three pounds a night in advance, was on the first floor back, and Celia paid her twelve pounds for four nights. She had the use of the bathroom at specified hours, and of the lavatory when vacant on the landing. She gave the name of Farr to the landlady, Mrs Harris.

'Will you be going out for a meal?' Mrs Harris asked her.

'No – I can't.'

'I don't do supper,' Mrs Harris explained.

'No – don't trouble yourself – I'm very tired.'

'I could give you a cup of tea.'

'That's kind. Thank you. I'll pay you, of course.'

'Are you all right, dear?'

'Yes – I will be – I promise not to be a nuisance.'

'I'll get you the tea.'

Celia lay on the lumpy bed in the cramped little room. Tea with two digestive biscuits arrived: she drank the tea and nibbled one of the biscuits. The light faded, night fell, the noise of traffic subsided, at last the milkmen rattled their bottles, dawn came to her rescue and morning began again.

She agreed to eat a boiled egg for her breakfast in Mrs Harris' neat kitchen. Afterwards she went out – the weather was grey but dry. She bought an envelope and a stamp, put the key of her Mini in the envelope, also a scrap of paper on which she wrote, 'Owen, My/your car is in the car park at Berkhamstead station. Thank you for marrying me.' She sealed the envelope, addressed it to Pennygate, stamped and posted it in Oxford Street.

She was trying to cover her tracks. She became aware that she was more likely to be recognised by Owen's friends and acquaintances in the West End than elsewhere, and headed north once more. She sat in Regent's Park, watching the grey squirrels. She bought a cheese and pickle sandwich from a stall – how different from the food she had eaten for lunch only yesterday! She had nothing to do.

At one o'clock she took the tube to Highgate. She had been doing her sums. A hundred and fifty pounds would have looked like a fortune to the Celia Farr of yore, but for Celia Pennant it had been the pettiest of petty cash. Now, for different reasons, it was scarcely adequate. She might have to buy something warm to wear and something rainproof. She might have to buy more strengthening food. She could last about a fortnight, counting contingencies. In Highgate, she walked to St Hugh's Hospital and asked if she could complete her training as a nurse there. St Hugh's and St Mildred's were connected somehow; she had once been posted from St Mildred's to work at St Hugh's for ten days of an epidemic. The office staff checked up on who she was and so on, and, no doubt because of staff shortages, granted her wish. She signed forms and was told to report at six o'clock on the next Sunday evening to Appleton House, accommodation for St Hugh's nurses.

That evening she rang her parents from another phone box and got through to her father.

She said: 'I've got a job, and I'll manage now. You needn't worry, Dad. I'm sorry if people are harassing you about me.' She added, because she could hear Chrissy screaming in the background: 'And I'm sorry to have upset Mother.'

He said: 'I'm so glad you've rung, my dear. Thank you for thinking of us. The people you mention wonder if you'd meet Sandy Wellingham.

Sandy's offered, she's very fond of you, and, if you wished, you could give her answers to the sort of questions I'm being asked.'

'Yes,' Celia agreed.

'Would you meet her?'

'When and where, Dad?'

'Wait a minute – yes, here it is – the bar of a small hotel called The Lytton in Wigmore Street behind Selfridges at eleven o'clock on Wednesday morning.'

'No tricks?'

'Sandy's promised me that no one else in the world has or will have the information I've just passed on.'

'Okay – I'll be there.'

Shortly afterwards, the money that Celia had paid for the call ran out.

In due course, after long intervening hours had dragged by, Celia kept the appointment.

The wan young woman and the smart brisk older lady embraced. Sandy ordered cups of coffee, and led the way to a table at the far end of the room.

'Do you want to tell a tale?' she asked.

'Not particularly, no.'

'Do you mind if I ask for guidance? Stop me if I'm too inquisitive or boring.'

'I will.'

'Have you any intention of going back to Owen?'

'No.'

'Ever?'

'Never.'

'I gather he was unfaithful?'

'With Mary-Ann Town.'

'That baggage!'

'Exactly.'

'He regrets it. He's miserable.'

'I can't be sorry for him. He broke his vows to me. I believed him and was wrong. I have nothing more to give him. I couldn't let him touch me again.'

'Some women can cope with the awfulness of their men.'

'I speak for myself.'

'No tears for Owen?'

'I do my crying at night.'

'You justify my faith in you, dear Celia. Forgive me for introducing you to a rotter. Poor girl! I sympathise with you exclusively. Brass tacks now – are you going to divorce Owen?'

'Yes – some time.'

'And blame him?'

'No.'

'You're entitled to take him to the cleaners.'

'I'm not keeping or taking any of his money. Here's our joint cheque book – will you return it to him?'

'You have a marriage settlement which belongs to you.'

'Not any more – it's his – he can have it – I won't be beholden – cancellation's the object of the exercise for me.'

'Is that a bit hasty?'

'No.'

'Owen can afford to discharge his debt to you.'

'There's no debt.'

'He should pay – he's always been allowed to get away with treating women badly. Don't ruin yourself financially, too.'

'I'm not going to be ruined. I can't let him ruin me. I didn't deserve to be treated as I have been. He must have told me a thousand times that I satisfied him physically. Tell him that I'd be grateful if he'd organise our divorce. He can settle the bill for that.'

'You won't change your mind? I don't want to carry a message you'll regret.'

'I won't regret it, Sandy.'

'Well – I was always fond of you – but I didn't know quite how exceptional you are – I can't say whether or not you're being wise, but I respect you, dear Celia, and I'll do your bidding. Concerning money – one word more – do you need any?'

'No, thanks.'

'I could lend you some.'

'No, honestly.'

'Ask me if you're ever short – I'd be flattered if you did.'

'Thanks again.'

'My Dot – your Dot – she's pining to see you, and Con ditto. Any chance of a get together?'

'Not yet. I'll have to settle into my job first.'

'You've got one already?'

'I have.'

'Good for you!'

'I'll have to leave you now.'

'I was hoping you might lunch with me?'

'I'm sorry, no – I've nothing much to do – but I don't want to talk any more about my situation – and I'm afraid I can't talk about anything else. Please understand! Sandy, one other favour – would you kindly give Owen my wedding ring and my engagement ring? Here they are. I haven't run off with any of the jewellery he gave me.'

'Oh dear! I can't help feeling sad.'

'I know – but there it is!'

They stood up, embraced, and Sandy patted Celia on the back until the latter turned and walked out of the bar with her face averted.

Two days later, again in the evening, she rang her home, hoping to speak to her father. Unfortunately her mother answered the call, and began to cry and curse.

Celia waited. She had known Chrissy would side with Owen, and say that she was being hard, cruel, unforgiving and foolish, but nonetheless she felt sick at heart.

Eventually the incoherence boiled down to a question: would Celia at least meet Owen and listen to what he had to say for himself?

'I wanted to talk to Dad about that. Is he there, Mother? I'll tell Dad,' she replied.

Chrissy complained, but, when Celia was silent, gave up and handed over the instrument.

Celia and her father hurried through the preliminaries, knowing time was limited.

'Dad, I can't resume more or less normal life until I know that Owen won't track me down or seek me out and try to put pressure on me.

I have nothing to say to him, and won't weaken or be persuaded. It's all over. Has he spoken to you?'

'Frequently. He wants to know where you are. As you haven't told me I can't tell him.'

'I need an undertaking or a guarantee that he's not going to persecute me. Could you try to explain to him?'

'Yes – but I don't know how dependable he'd be.'

'There are legal injunctions, aren't there, to stop one person persecuting another?'

'Oh, I don't think it would or should come to that.'

'No. Owen would agree with you. That's why I'd go for it if the worst came to the worst.'

'I'll make him see sense.'

'Thank you, Dad. I'm sending you my love, Dad.'

'Same here!'

Celia had paid Mrs Harris for three extra nights of her stay, Thursday, Friday and Saturday. They had become friendly by the Saturday evening. Mrs Harris had not only continued to give Celia evening cups of tea, but had often provided a jam or ham sandwich as well as the biscuit. She was more motherly than Chrissy had ever been, and was concerned that Celia looked 'peaky' and 'down'.

On the Sunday morning they reminded each other that Celia was having her final breakfast. Mrs Harris said that she would be missed, and Celia gave her twenty of her remaining forty pounds to cover the extras.

82

'Oh no, please – I was never one for charging for nothing.'

'Of course not – but I'd like to give you a present in my turn – I'll have other money after today.'

Mrs Harris was duly grateful, then asked: 'May I ask you a question, Miss? It's personal.'

'I'll answer if I can,' Celia replied.

'Is it a convent you're going to?'

Celia laughed.

'No, nothing like that, I'm not cut out to be a nun. I came to your house because of my marriage, because of the end of it.'

'Oh, I'm sorry.'

'So am I.'

'Did you love him, dear?'

'Yes, once. You lost your husband, you told me, but he died.'

'He was called John – Johnny, we called him.'

'Were you happy with Johnny, Mrs Harris?'

'We were married for thirty-four years, and we were happy as the day is long. I don't think we had words more than once or twice, and it was always kiss and make up with us.'

'Did you have children?'

'No, dear. I had a miscarriage early on, and that was that. It was a pity, and might have been a sadness to Johnny, but we were closer because two's company, and he never showed me he had regrets.'

'What did Johnny do?'

'He repaired antique furniture. He was a

83

cabinet-maker by trade. He was a good carver. He was a good man.'

'Did you live with him in this house?'

'Oh yes. We saved to buy it. We were proud to own the house, we were. Johnny wouldn't leave it – for holidays, I mean. We did day-trips to Brighton sometimes, but we were both happier to be here quietly, laughing and making improvements. Thirty-four years wasn't a day too much. I've loved Johnny just the same every day since he died.'

Celia cried. She sobbed and the great tears ran down her cheeks and splashed on the breakfast table or her lap. She cried on and off for the rest of the morning and in the afternoon until it was time to kiss Mrs Harris goodbye.

PART TWO

Four years have passed. Celia, who has reclaimed her maiden surname, is twenty-eight. Her paternal grandfather, her GranFarr who lived at Westgate-on-Sea, is no more. Bernard Farr, her father, has retired, and her mother Chrissy is no longer fit – she has a wonky hip and now complains mostly of pain. Bernard is a patient husband and the most undemanding of loving fathers: he attends functions at The Welcome School, reads books and studies his seabirds. Constance Thornton, formerly Shelby, has two children, Jessie and Jake – Celia and Dot Wellingham are Jessica's godmothers. Dot has a flatlet of her own in London, she has moved out of the Pimlico Road house, where Geoffrey Wellingham has his antique shop and he and Sandy occupy the upper floors. Dot is not married, but involved with a man who is – no, not the collector. She works full-time in her father's shop.

Celia is a State Registered Nurse employed by St Hugh's Hospital in Highgate – she finished her training there and stayed on. She is buying a flat within walking distance of her work. She has lost her girlish twinkle and the tensed slenderness of healthy young women. She is mature now, curvaceous, strong. Her nurse's uniform suits her, the headgear adds attractions to her neat blonde hair, and the buckled belt accentuates her small waist. Her complexion is fresh, her smile ready, her teeth nice to look at, her blue eyes wide and unflinching, and her regard steady and receptive, a trifle sceptical but not cynical.

She was very cut up by her divorce from Owen Pennant. She hated people thinking or hinting that he had broken her heart. She insisted inwardly and sometimes outwardly that he was a womaniser, not a heart-breaker. She was disillusioned and felt foolish when she overcame the sense of outrage. She was aware that the world would either think she should not have married Owen; or that she should have put up with the common lot of wives injured by their husbands' infidelity and sexual peccadilloes; or that she should have punished the adulterer financially. Chrissy, contrarily, reproached her daughter for not 'fleecing' her ex-son-in-law and former favourite.

For ages Owen refused to take no for an answer. In messages sent via Sandy Wellingham he demanded reconciliation and at least a meeting. He apologised and threatened. Then he begged her to pocket the money on offer, that was hers by rights. His final note on the subject ran: 'Okay – please yourself and my bank manager. I can't be sorry for ever.'

Celia had a spot of trouble with her best friends. Referring to the divorce laws and speaking as a trader born and bred, Dot could hardly bear to think of what was slipping through Celia's fingers. Con, who could see nothing wrong with money for jam, began by ranting at Owen and then ranted at Celia.

The three of them met in the fullness of time in Dot's flat in the cheaper end of Pimlico. The question and answer session regarding Celia's marriage began at the beginning.

The romance seemed to have been a whirlwind, why was that, considering Celia's cautious attitude to the opposite sex?

'He forced the pace,' she explained. 'It was kisses after the charity ball. I tried to apply brakes, but he was in the driving seat. He wanted it all, he wanted to sleep with me, and you can't ask a man like Owen to wait. I didn't want to lose him. I wanted to sleep with him, too.'

'Couldn't you have had him on approval?' Dot asked.

'I was set on being a virgin bride. I know it sounds Victorian but there it is – or was. And I knew in my bones and everywhere else that once I'd tried him out or tried him on I wouldn't be returning him to sender.'

'What was the honeymoon like? You looked so happy after it.'

'I was happy. We seemed to me to be made for each other. It was all lessons in love. It was an all-action movie. Our talk was baby-talk really. I can't remember any conversation or even much exchange of information. I think he's a Protestant, anyway we were married in a Church of England church.'

'Don't you wish you'd known him better?'

'My wishes had come true.'

'What happened when the kissing stopped?'

'It never stopped completely. But he was either

89

churning out money or socialising, and I had Pennygate and Eaton Square to run. Our life was like a film that's winding on ahead of itself.'

'Why no baby?'

'I've got something wrong with my Fallopian tubes.'

Con had experience of Fallopian tubes. She said hers had been tested: the doctor had compared them to Welcome Hall.

Then she asked Celia: 'Were yours blocked?'

'Apparently, according to my doctor, and evidently also.'

'Didn't you have them seen to?'

'No. I did nothing, which was odd, because we weren't getting on badly, and I knew the operation was straightforward. I was longing to be a mother, and I had no idea that we might split up. Subconsciously, I must have been prepared for something to go wrong.'

Dot and Con wondered about the last chapter of Celia's story: 'Don't tell us if you don't want to.'

'I don't mind. We've always shared our secrets. We had people to stay the weekend at Pennygate, including Mary-Ann Town. On the Sunday afternoon I heard a noise in a room that wasn't occupied and investigated. Owen sat in a chair facing me and Mary-Ann was on her knees. She scrambled to her feet and said something unattractive as she left the room. Owen sat there looking at me – he was doing up his trousers, but still in the grip, if you catch my meaning. He looked at me without seeing me while he enjoyed himself – and that described Owen as a husband to a t. There was nothing left to hang about for, and never would be.'

Celia continued: 'I suppose I'm puritanical. I thought my marriage meant as much to Owen as it did to me. He proved he didn't think so, and it didn't, so our marriage was a lost cause by my standards.'

Dot said: 'Well, I understand you, I admire you, I've realised how serious your serious side is, but I'm afraid I wouldn't have done as you've done – I'd have eaten crow and humble pie and all those disgusting things.'

Con said: 'You're so brave, Celia.'

Some months later the friends met again, and Con asked Celia if she was feeling better and if by chance there was anybody else.

'Yes and no,' Celia replied. 'I am better, and I'm not looking at men. I shan't for years, if ever. But I must say that men in London, and at St Hugh's hospital in particular, look at women far more than they did at St Mildred's in Canterbury, or in Kent for that matter.'

She gave satirical accounts of recent propositions put to her by the medical profession. One of the surgeons at St Hugh's had asked if she would be excited by him wearing his rubber gloves. Another had suggested making love to her while she was strapped into the gynaecological chair. A large nurse of military bearing had put forward a plan for them to spend an afternoon together. And patients were worse. A man with his broken leg suspended from a sling had asked her to do something gymnastic for him. Lots of men asked more or less misleadingly to be kissed good night. Bed baths were never given by one nurse to invalids of the opposite sex – two nurses were meant to be safe, and the same applied to male nurses bathing women. As for 'mixed' wards for patients of both sexes, only a politician could have dreamed up such an unpleasant and impractical proposal.

The three girls' reunions were not devoted exclusively to the study of Celia's love-life. Con spoke of Ian Thornton in unflattering terms that were contradicted by her contented appearance. She had formed a habit of calling Ian old – her 'old' Ian, her 'poor old fool of a hubby', her 'old boy' and so on – although he was actually thirty-six: the word 'old' was clearly an endearment in her terminology. She said that the best thing about her marriage was not having to take a hot water bottle to bed in the winter. She said Ian was 'frightfully' law-abiding, and 'lost his rag' if she drove faster than the speed limit or tasted a grape in a shop to discover if the bunch was worth buying.

Con was a doting mother, and produced photographs of her offspring. Jessie, Celia and Dot's god-daughter, was unphotogenic or else lumpy and plain, and Jake looked a hundred years old in his cot. Con retailed their sayings and harped on their winning ways, but said, 'No more, they're the last of the Shelby-Thorntons.' She confessed she was sick of sex, and had chosen to take complicated precautions in hopes of putting Ian off. But after all, as she would wind up her reports to her friends, she was a lucky devil, since her 'funny old dear was on his feet and just about compos', and her little ones had a full complement of fingers and toes.

Dot's situation was more complex. After her virginity had been 'collected' by that collector, she fell for a married man with the typically difficult wife. She had made the mistake of allowing him to cry on her shoulder, sympathised with his tales of woe, offered him the treat of herself in an attempt to cheer him up, and discovered that she had become the pig in the middle of his marriage. 'I'm not his mistress, I'm hardly an adulteress, I'm nothing romantic or wicked,' she informed her friends ruefully. 'No – I'm a ragged old sticking plaster, and can't pull myself off for fear of more blood on the carpet.'

Celia and Con assured her that one day a wandering knight on a white horse would ride by and throw her across his saddle-bow: at which Dot laughingly reminded them of her height and weight.

Talking of wandering knights on a later occasion, in the second year of Celia's divorced status, she asked Dot and Con what they had really made of Owen.

Con said he had frightened her, he had reminded her of Johnny-head-in-air, he was haughty and impolite.

Dot said: 'He made my inferiority complex worse. When we shook hands he showed me I wasn't his type, and I knew he wasn't mine.'

Dot and Con together wished they had warned Celia to take it easy and not to be rushed off her feet.

Celia answered: 'It wouldn't have made a scrap of difference if you had.'

But two and a half years after her divorce, in the course of another session with her two friends she regaled them with the following story.

'I saw Owen from the top of a bus the other day. He was talking to another man on the pavement of the road running down from Hyde Park Corner to Victoria Station. I was sitting in the front seat of the upper deck of the bus. I thought he must be a male model or a film star before I recognised him. He wore a grey suit – Savile Row – long double-breasted jacket – light grey flannel – I remembered it, and I remember him talking about his expensive clothes, how they were made, how they had to look. He had an athlete's physique, clothes looked wonderful on him, and he knew it and carried a fortune on his back. He was the man I and others fell in love with. He had that beguiling sharp attentive expression on his face, reserved for women he didn't know well and wanted to know better, and for men who might help him to make more money. Don't pity me! I was immune. He inspired mild interest, nothing else. I was so glad I'd done what I did and was not his wife.'

To start with Celia had missed sex. But at St Hugh's she tended invalids and eased suffering,

94

she was coping with other people's emotions as best she could, and before long she seemed to have no time for her own. Besides, she was resistant to any sort of involvement.

At some stage she noticed she was more restless than she had been. She found it difficult to concentrate on reading books or on radio or TV when she was alone in her flat. At the same time she was touched by a tragic story unfolding in the hospital. A young woman who was chronically ill had also been pregnant, her baby had been delivered but had then died, the mother was a terminal case and the husband was desperate.

Celia had known worse situations. This one was different for all the nursing staff because the mother, May Sturridge, was so charming and sweet, and her husband Alan was such a dignified gentleman. Celia, on night duty, met and talked to Alan Sturridge.

He was tall and had a long face. He was in his forties and had a good head of dark hair going grey. May Sturridge was the only patient in a four-bedded room. Alan at night was allowed to sit with her far beyond visiting hours. When she slept with the aid of drugs, he would stretch his legs or drink a cup of tea or coffee in an empty annexe to the main ward. Celia, waiting to attend to May, would sometimes talk or listen to Alan there.

He was a solicitor and worked in the branch of a big firm in Stanmore. He said he was not a high-flyer, he did the conveyancing; he had been brought up in the country, and felt he was more a countryman than a guttersnipe. May was thirty years of age. They had been married for four years, postponed starting a family, then May fell ill yet managed to conceive their child. If the child had lived, Alan was sure May would not be dying. As it was, he blamed himself – the strain of pregnancy, the effort of labour, had exhausted her strength to fight against her disease.

Celia said: 'Who knows?'

He said she was comforting. He uttered paeans of praise of his wife, her beauty, her intelligence, her humour and humanity. They had lived the quietest of lives, for each other, and spent their holidays in England, by the sea, in Cornwall and Devon, in East Anglia. He dreaded widowerhood. What would he do with himself? He despaired of ever getting over the loss of May, his well-named better half, the spirit of springtime.

Celia mentioned her experience that slotted in towards the other end of the scale of matrimonial satisfaction, and he was unselfish enough to sympathise.

One night he cursed God, and she commented, 'If in doubt, kick the Almighty.' He asked her if she believed in God, and she answered, 'Yes – I was taught God, and He's a help when you're in trouble, whether or not He created the trouble in the first place. But I expect I've shaped my God to suit myself – everybody does.'

He sought further explanation.

'Oh well,' she laughed, 'my religion's about happiness. I think we have to pray to God to let us be happy – even happy again. I can't believe God's impressed by unhappiness, although some people are determined that He is, our Christian God is, aren't they?'

'What a difficult creed!'

'Sorry,' she said.

'Don't be! Thank you.'

May Sturridge died the day after the night in which Celia and Alan spoke of religion.

Some weeks later Celia buttonholed Mr Gibson, the gynaecologist, in a corridor at the hospital. They were acquaintances, and had a jokey relationship.

'Would you like to cut me up?' she asked.

'Don't tempt me,' he replied.

The consequence was an appointment in his consulting room. She was scolded for having done nothing about her Fallopian tubes for so long. An urgent x-ray examination followed, then an operation. It was successful. She recuperated for a few days at Broadstairs and returned to work.

Then Celia received a letter from Alan Sturridge. He had sent it to St Hugh's. She was relieved to see that the writing on the envelope was not Owen's – she did not recognise the writing. Seeing Alan's name was a shock.

The letter ran: 'Dear Celia, I wonder if you would or could have tea with me at the Queen's Head hotel next Friday? I have work in Highgate on that day, and would like to thank you again for your kindness when my wife was ill. Drop a line to my office, as above.'

The writing paper was headed Carter Johnssen,

Solicitors, and the office was in Stanmore. Celia wrote back that she had a free hour between four and five o'clock on Friday, and looked forward to seeing Alan.

The Queen's Head in Highgate had once been a coaching inn. The two reception rooms where tea was served were small and dark, but quite cosy with wood fires smouldering on piles of ash in the blackened fireplaces. Alan sat at a table in the farther room – nobody else was present. He shook her hand and rang for tea and biscuits. He looked better, less drawn, than he had in the hospital.

Their talk was impersonal. They asked after each other's health. They touched on work, holidays, plans for the future if any, friends and family. His father was dead, he had an ailing mother in a residential home in Stanmore, and a sister married to a Swede, the mother of two, living in Stockholm but in poor health. She described Broadstairs, and she poured the tea.

In the last ten minutes of their hour he launched into a panegyric of May, and said how much he was missing her. Celia almost had to interrupt in order to say goodbye. He apologised for talking too much. She said he had not and thanked him. When they shook hands no second meeting was suggested.

She had not expected much more. She was hardly disappointed – she would not agree that he attracted her. She was just sorry for him, they were friendly acquaintances. And she suspected that, for all his talk of May, he was an unromantic chap, and inhibited. Nevertheless she had jumped to see his signature on the letter, and she had thought of him occasionally in the preceding months, ever since their nocturnal confabs in the hospital.

She had a more concrete worry. She had been shy with him in the Queen's Head. She was forced against her will to compare him with Owen, who knew too well how to excite a woman without making her feel uneasy. She had not been shy with Alan while May was alive. As a nurse she mixed with men. She had seen off members of the opposite sex who wanted to lay hands on her body, and made comrades of others. Now, aged twenty-eight and an ex-wife, she had not been able to meet Alan's simple and sincere blue eyes. She was annoyed by the effect he had on her, whatever it was, and resolved not to think of him any more.

But a month later another letter arrived. They drank more tea and ate more biscuits at the Queen's Head. This time he asked her to lunch – it had to be a month ahead – she had duties in Broadstairs, he was visiting his sister in Sweden. The lunch passed pleasantly, and they agreed to meet a third time: which was no use in any emotional sense.

Their fourth meeting was lunch on a Saturday. Alan fetched Celia from the hospital at noon, drove her to Stanmore in his car – not a Mercedes-Benz, a Morris Minor, he told her – and after lunch in a Chinese restaurant to meet his mother. Mrs Sturridge was a nice old lady; but Celia was

not pleased to deduce that Alan had subjected
her to inspection by his mother, who would tell
him how far to venture along the primrose path.
He should be capable of deciding if he wanted
to make love and to whom, she thought. She
also took exception to the possibility that he
might be thinking of marriage before he had
held her hand or kissed her even on the cheek
– what was he – cold, restrained by snobbery
of some description, lazy, homosexual? Yet May
had died partly because of the baby he had given
her.

They met another time or two. Her shyness
was yielding to a challenging mood. She was too
old for platonic friendship, and could not hang
about for ever while he was in mourning. When
he deposited her back at the hospital after another
lunch at Stanmore, she kissed him. He had
opened the door of the Minor to let her alight,
he was strong on the gentlemanly gesture, and
she reached up and kissed him in the region of
his ear. He was startled – at least he looked
round in a startled fashion – there was a small
crowd of people arriving or leaving near the
hospital entrance. He might have been embarrassed.

'Don't worry,' she laughed, 'I'll tell the gossips
you're my brother.'

He laughed too, exclaimed 'No!' as if to deny
something or other, he also mentioned the date
of their next meeting, and she waved goodbye.

She wondered if that kiss would be a turning
point. But nothing turned. The only change was

that he kissed her on the cheek at the beginning and the end of their time together. She did not really care. She liked him – he was a decent kind sensible man, and rang much truer than Owen. She admired him, valued his friendship, thought she could see through him, and was sorry he was sad.

Their meetings continued. It crossed Celia's mind that her relationship with Alan was neutralising her attractions for the opposite sex in general. Time kept on passing, and her readiness for love merged with impatience. Out of the blue a third letter from Alan reached her.

'Dear Celia,' he wrote in his regular legible hand; 'A while ago you said you could pass me off as your brother. I know it was a joke, but I have never felt like your brother. Please forgive me if I have been slow to show that my feelings for you are of a different colour – you know the reason, I'm sure. At last my previous life seems to have set me free. Ever since I met you in St Hugh's Hospital I have admired you. At first you were my nurse as well as May's, and my comforter. I loved you in those roles, and then as an unattached man I grew to love you more and more. I would, if you permitted it, love you in the ultimate way, and devote the rest of my life to making you as happy as possible. I am presumptuous to be writing in this strain, for I am well aware that you are far above me in many respects, but I believe your modesty and kindness will let you read on. I am asking you to marry me. I know I don't deserve you.

Tell me if I can hope. I shall not be a nuisance to you if your answer's no. Dearest Celia, all for now. Alan.'

She had Alan's office and home telephone numbers. She could have rung him immediately. Instead she wrote him the following note in the evening.

'Dearest Alan, Thank you thank you – I'm grateful for ever! My heart is touched and I'm prouder than peacocks. Give me a little time, please! It's Monday today, we've got a date on Saturday, could you wait till then? Loose ends to be tied up, nothing personal. With my love, C.'

She could have added crosses representing kisses, but did not. She posted her note with a sigh that expressed unaccountable contradictory emotions. She wanted a man, marriage, children, and that sort of security. She knew Alan filled the bill almost to perfection, and she was fond of him. But his letter had been a trifle dry, self-centred too. He put her on a pedestal and grovelled in the dust at her feet. Could she live up to the standards he was setting? Would he be fun to live with? And how good would he be at loving?

The telephone call she did make was to Dot. She called for an urgent consultation with both her friends with luck, with one or the other at least. Dot rang back to say that Con was 'tied by the leg' by her 'blasted kids', and that she herself would report to St Hugh's in Celia's lunch hour on the Tuesday.

'What's wrong?' she asked.

'Marriage.'

'What's wrong with that?'

'You'll have to tell me what's right.'

They met at twelve-thirty. They ate sandwiches and drank beakers of tea in Dot's mini – Celia had bought the food in the canteen.

She gave Dot a full account of Alan's courtship, and tried to describe his outward appearance and his character.

'He doesn't sound wrong to me,' Dot said.

'I don't know.'

'What don't you know?'

'I fell for such a different sort of man before, and might again.'

'You don't hanker after another cad?'

'No no no.'

'Why then!'

'I'm afraid of hurting Alan. I'm afraid of making another mistake. I'm afraid he may be too poor, just as Owen was too rich. I'm afraid of being contrary. And I don't know how to wriggle out.'

'My father says, "When in doubt do nowt".'

'I can't do nowt.'

'Your children could wait.'

'True!'

'Where would you live with Alan?'

'Not where he lived with May. We haven't got down to a single brass tack.'

'You're a good earner, Celia.'

'I wouldn't be if I was a mother.'

'Con's message to you was not to miss the bus.'

103

'Con's so adaptable. What about you, Dot? I've done all the talking – sorry!'

'I'm plugging along, and listening for the sound of horse's hoofs.'

'Are you still the sticking plaster?'

'I'm determined to get unstuck. I mean, it's not logical – I love a man who loves me, we wish we were married, but the love he receives from me weighs on his conscience and makes him more uxorious, he says he can't desert his frigid little wife, so I'm my own worst enemy and ruin my chances.'

Dot also said she was ashamed of committing adultery.

'I blush at the most inconvenient moments when I remember Owen and that Town woman, and your reaction,' she confessed.

Celia replied: 'You haven't made the solemn vows that Owen broke.'

They circled round their dilemmas, and discussed the various methods of tying the knot.

Dot said: 'I wouldn't care how it was tied as long as it was tied quickly. The last thing I want is my man wandering around without having promised to be mine. I'd lock him in if I could.'

'Alan wouldn't have to promise anything much because we'd be marrying in a Register Office,' Celia reflected. 'But he's not a wanderer. Oh dear!'

'What would I think of him?' Dot asked.

'You'd think he was charming, but a bit of a stick, a charming stick.'

'Have you slept with him?'

'Not yet.'

'That might settle it.'

'Yes.'

On the Wednesday Celia was torn almost in two by pros and cons, and on Thursday she rang her father. She told him her story so far as it went in hopes that he would tell her the inevitable ending. But her hesitancy influenced him to recommend caution.

'Time will decide, play for time, my dear.'

'But we're not playing, Dad – Alan's the opposite of a playboy.'

'I'm glad to hear it. Bring him down to see us. You've met his mother.'

'I haven't met his sister.'

'His sister's married with children and lives in Stockholm, she has more to worry about than her brother's second wife.'

Celia laughed.

Bernard wound up their conversation by saying: 'Remember your problem's a problem of success.'

Friday was again devoted to pros and cons, neither of which would yield to the other; and on Saturday she finished at the hospital at noon and returned to her flat by way of the shops.

She had decided to entertain Alan at home, rather than to be taken to dinner at the Chinese restaurant they frequented. She bought small fillet steaks, baking potatoes and salad, cheddar cheese, apples and peppermint creams, also a bottle of red wine that ought to be good considering the price, and a posy of flowers. There was no dining-room in her flat – it consisted of sitting-room, bedroom, bathroom and kitchen: the occasional guests she had cooked for had balanced their plates of food on their knees. Alan would be the first person she would entertain formally. She cleared space between the sofa and two armchairs, removed objects from the top of the table standing against the wall, pulled it into the open space, laid it with side plates, cutlery, wine glasses and tumblers, and placed the vase containing her posy of white roses and greenery between the settings. For chairs to sit on at dinner, she rescued one from the bedroom and the other from the hallway near the telephone.

She then had a bath, slightly made up her face for a change, did what she could to her hair, dressed in her best silky garment and waited.

The doorbell rang at seven-thirty precisely. For one more time Celia wondered how to greet Alan and what on earth to say to him. She opened the door and looked up into the eyes of the large man awkwardly carrying a bunch of flowers. His expression was nervous verging on hangdog. She had to cheer him up, and she threw her arms wide and embraced him.

'Come in,' she said, holding his hand and shutting the door. 'Come in, dear Alan – you've brought me flowers, thank you – let me take your coat and your cap – that's it – come and sit down!'

'What a very nice greeting,' he said.

She asked him to uncork the wine while she put his flowers in water. They sat side by side on the sofa, clinked glasses and drank, and he said the wine was excellent.

'Oh Alan,' she said, 'forgive me for keeping you on tenterhooks. But I will explain. We've so much to talk about I don't know where to start. I've arranged dinner here – you'll have to forgive my cooking, too. How are you? Are you well?'

'I think so, I hope so – all the better for seeing you.'

'You see me, but you haven't heard what I have to say.'

'Is it no?'

'No –'

'Oh Celia!'

'Not really no, but not quite yes.'

'I'll have to fortify myself with the wine.'

'We both have stories to tell each other.'

'I suppose we do, although I've had the feeling that you've always understood me.'

'Shall I see to things in the kitchen? The potatoes take about another half-hour to bake.'

'A capital idea!'

She left him on the sofa for a few minutes, during which she also marinated the steaks and put the cheese on a plate.

She returned and asked: 'How much do you know about my marriage and divorce?'

'Very little.'

'My husband was Owen Pennant. He's a millionaire. He's handsome and roughly ten years older than me. We married in haste – and marriage proved the point that he was not right for me. We had two homes and an army of servants – our life was a social roundabout, which

107

made me giddy – too many people crowding in, too many lit candles, and he put business first. If I'm complaining of the life we led, I shouldn't – lots of girls long to live in a glamorous whirl. Have you met people such as I'm trying to describe?'

'I can't say I have, and I can't imagine that you would have enjoyed the whirling.'

'No – but it might have become more acceptable. The key to Owen's character is greed – but, again, I shouldn't run him down now, because once I thought he was okay. He taught me a lot of lessons.'

'I daresay, but ...'

'There were two buts. He grew tired of me or tireder, and he liked the look of the grass in another garden. Are you with me, Alan?'

'Was he unfaithful?'

'I caught him out.'

'I'm sorry.'

'I lost faith in him.'

'No doubt.'

'I divorced him, but I have none of his money – no alimony, and his presents to me returned. I live on my nurse's salary.'

'I imagined so, but thank you for telling me.'

'What I specially wanted you to know is that divorce equals sin in my opinion, and even crime if children are involved. It always did, and still does. I'm not immoral or permissive or whatever they call it. Some people said I was hard on Owen to divorce him for a single act of adultery. My reasoning was that he had been unfaithful within mere months of marrying me, in my house, under my nose almost, and that I wouldn't be prepared to bear his children. I couldn't see the point of asking for trouble. Owen treated me wrong not only by his sexual behaviour, also by forcing me to sin by divorcing him. My heart isn't hard, it was awfully bruised by the whole business, and that's why I feel I can't rush into saying yes to you. Please...'

'Please don't apologise, Celia, my dear. I wouldn't rush you for the world. My opinion is that you behaved heroically to draw a line through your marriage and begin all over again.'

She kissed him. She leant across and kissed him – on the cheek – by way of thanks. He looked a little startled, as before. They both laughed, there was some small talk, and then she asked him a question.

'Would you like to talk about your marriage?'

'There's not much to tell that you don't already know. May was a sweet girl. Truthfully, she died before she had fully grown up. Our marriage had pain in it, owing to her illness.'

'Is it terribly painful to remember her?'

'Not so painful as it was. I've come to terms with it. I wouldn't have proposed to you if I hadn't felt free.'

She was grateful and sympathetic. They agreed that they were lucky to have found each other. She went into the kitchen to prepare dinner.

They ate at the table. They swapped memories of their childhoods and schooling. He had been called up into the army post-war and won a commission; but he served in office jobs because of injuring his back on an assault course – the back had cured itself. He aspired to become a barrister, but his father died young, the family was short of money, so he had to settle for the shorter and cheaper course of legal studies that qualified him to be a solicitor and breadwinner. He believed his job with Carter Johnssen was secure. He said he was forty-seven years old. Celia described Broadstairs, Thanet Steps, her parents, her two best friends, St Mildred's Hospital and St Hugh's. She said she was twenty-nine.

After dinner they returned to the sofa. They had chatted amicably; but the tension underneath was tightening. As he made no move in her direction, she put her arm round his neck, pulled his head towards her and kissed him on the lips. The kiss was disturbingly polite – nothing like those kisses to which Owen had accustomed her. When they drew apart, she smiled at him as if to challenge, and he said the kiss had been wonderful but that it was getting late and should he not be going?

'Stay here tonight,' she said.

'Would you like me to?'

'Yes. Wouldn't you?'

'I would indeed.'

They went in turn to the bathroom. He went first. She turned on no lights, and arranged the bed-covers invitingly. As he emerged from the bathroom, she kissed him again in passing.

He was not in bed when she re-entered the bedroom. He was sitting on the side of the bed, in his tweed jacket, collar, tie and trousers. She sat beside him and discovered he was trembling. She patted him on the back, said it would be all right, wondered momentarily if she ought to suggest postponement, yearned against her will for a touch of Owen's proficiency, and decided to forge ahead. Alan was mumbling apologies. She helped him out of his jacket and knelt to undo the laces of his shoes – she undressed him bit by bit.

'Come into bed,' she said. 'Don't worry!'

She almost bundled him in, then dropped her knickers and climbed in beside him. The bed was single and narrow. It was shaking for the wrong reason. They were clamped unavoidably close, but he offered her no caress. She felt it would be an affront to him to take charge and undignified for her. Besides, he was like an ill person: she could only kiss him gently on his forehead now and then.

He spoke in broken accents of his difficulties with May. She had hated the physical side, and not let him consummate their marriage for years. He could not be natural with her, he had lost his nerve, and, he feared, his capability. May's baby was conceived against the odds, and her attitude to pregnancy weakened her immune system. He had loved her for her youthfulness, and the worst thing had been her unpreparedness for death. Almost her last words were that she was setting him free, but, evidently, he was not free, not so free as he had hoped he was.

He loved Celia, he said repeatedly. He loved

her too much. He rambled on, as Celia had heard tell that men do in such situations – there were jokes about it in the women's wards. She found him a tissue with which to wipe his eyes. She begged him to calm down, and offered him a cup of tea, which he refused. She said truthfully that he was tired, that they both were. She told him not to say sorry again. Finally she said she was going to have a nap, kissed him good night and turned over as best she could and snuggled down.

She had sounded cheerful for his sake, but now she surrendered to pessimism. She could not marry Alan. She was not a sex fiend; but the reasons why she could not be the wife of a sexless husband were innumerable. It was a shame: Alan was lovely in the other ways. She had almost made a second mistake, she was angry with herself, humiliated, and tonight's fiasco would be difficult to forget. Furthermore, while considering her own best interests she remembered Alan's: if she married him compassionately, she would end by venting her frustration and scorning him.

She was very unhappy. She was going to have to look elsewhere for a mate. Her tiredness was no exaggeration: she had had a busy day and stress galore. She tried not to feel hostile towards the great lump of a silent man occupying most of the space in her bed.

She must have fallen asleep. She was woken by Alan turning. He was breathing in a manner she recognised, and touching her with a warm hand. She was instantly excited. She moved a little in order to help him. When they cried out in unison, she could hear his sorrows, her regrets, and their embarrassment drifting away in the sound.

They thanked each other, laughing. He whispered something about marriage in her ear.

'Well, well...' she replied, and then: 'Alan, I took no precautions.'

Celia Farr was aware that one swallow does not make a summer. Alan Sturridge was aware of it, too. They were both encouraged by their first night together, encouraged to verify and gather proof. They tried again on Sunday; made dates to meet in the nearest future; as the weeks passed he gained confidence, not only appeared to be manly, and she was reassured.

But there was a new uncertainty in the back of Celia's mind. Her Fallopian tubes were not in perfect condition. She banned the topic of matrimony, hoped and prayed for a month. She longed for a baby, they both did; at the same time she was afraid of disappointing Alan, who had already lost the child May had conceived, also unwilling to subject him to a wife having to undergo gynaecological help and probable surgery. Even when she missed one menstrual period she hesitated, and did not inform Alan in case it should turn out to be another single swallow.

One weekend she dared to introduce him to her parents. They went to stay the night at 42

Thanet Steps. Alan drove Celia down on the Saturday afternoon. They all had tea together, then he had gone off to spend half an hour with an ancient cousin who lived in Folkestone.

Bernard Farr congratulated his daughter without reservations. Alan Sturridge was what – or who – he had always hoped for: straightforward, decent, and no fool. Of course he did not know Alan well, but he was a schoolmaster and had spent his whole life assessing boys, their characters, their destinies. He knew a good thing when he saw one. And Celia's particular gratification was that her father enthused about her new lover as he had never done about her old one, despite Owen's charm and wealth.

Her mother was doubly contrary: she vocally regretted Owen, whom she had loved, then hated. She approved of Alan with a sniff, but could not help saying that he was no Prince Charming. She wanted to know if Celia and Alan were living in sin. Supposing they married, would there be money to pay the bills, would Celia have to carry on nursing, and had she any idea of the expense of raising a family, even a family with an only child, as had been her mother's lot? Marriage to Alan would obviously not be the Easy Street that it had been with Owen, Celia was warned.

Alan's return was like the repudiation of Chrissy's diatribe. He was so large and strong. He was calm and convincing. The evening passed pleasantly, and ended in separate bedrooms for the visitors – Alan had the spare room, Celia was in her childhood bedroom in the attic. On Sunday Bernard took Celia and Alan to the Communion Service at St Mary's, and Alan for a walk after breakfast. Goodbyes followed Sunday lunch.

The weather was not good. Broadstairs would not have been Broadstairs without a breeze being wafted down from Russia via the North Sea, but today the breeze was not far removed from a gale. Celia loved it – in North London she had missed her hair being almost blown away. She asked Alan if he would mind parking the Minor for five minutes in a back street near the sea front – not too close, since the salt spume and spray from the breaking waves would strip his car of paint. He agreed. They got out of the car and struggled to reach and cling on to a railing along the esplanade. They laughed at the force of the wind, looked at each other laughing, and watched the white horses in the distance and the mountainous waves crashing on to the shore and rocks and the swirling clouds of foam. Her nose and cheeks were red, and his tie had blown over his shoulder.

'I love you,' he shouted at her.

'I love you,' she shouted back, but he pretended not to hear and made her repeat it for all she was worth.

'Won't you marry me?' he asked.

'What?' she said, laughing and lying.

'Marry me, Celia!'

'All right.'

'Did you say all right?'

115

'I did.'

'Is it yes?'

'Yes yes yes yes!'

They kissed. They sealed their bargain with a kiss, and they had to hold on to each other in order not to fall or be blown apart on the way back to the Minor.

That evening Celia was on night duty. She parted with Alan outside her block of flats – she had telephone calls to make as well as to get ready to report at St Hugh's, and he also wanted to tell people how happy he was.

She rang her father first, then Con, then Dot.

Her conversation with Dot went beyond congratulations.

'What cured your qualms?' Dot asked.

'Guess!'

'Was it my advice?'

'Yes.'

'Was all well in that area?'

'Fine – and fine ever since.'

'As good as Owen?'

'Oh no – Alan's not a pro – but he gives more, he gives himself.'

'Lucky you!'

'Yes.'

'Your luck the first time round turned out to be bad luck.'

'Yes.'

'Why the monosyllables? Is there something I don't know?'

'I might be luckier still, and it frightens me.'

'What do you mean?'

116

'I'll tell you next month.'

'Oh that! Does Alan know?'

'He will when I'm quite sure.'

'Listen, I don't want to sound like your Dutch aunt, but luck does seem to go bad quickly, so you'd better enjoy it while it's good.'

'Thanks, Dot – you're right. How are you? How's the sticking plaster?'

'Unstuck – and I'm fancy free – and Mum's taking me to Paris for shopping in a fortnight.'

'You might buy a French husband in a shop.'

'*Peut-être!*'

Celia again followed Dot's advice. She had lovely new things to think about. Happiness and her work excluded retrograde wishes and futuristic anxieties. She and Alan met whenever they could, and he bought her an engagement ring of a garnet nestling amongst pearls, and she bought him a pigskin wallet. They discussed their wedding. She was against marrying again where she had married before, that is in Broadstairs, and felt the same about Alan and May's Stanmore. They compromised on Hampstead. As for the reception, it would have to be in a hotel or restaurant – her flat was too far from Hampstead and too small, and his presented other difficulties, since it had been the home of May Sturridge, and Celia had an aversion to trespassing there.

They fixed the date, and settled on a restaurant that specialised in such functions – neither of the couple-to-be had ever eaten there. Celia invited Con, Jessie and Jake to stay with her for the night before the wedding – Dot lived within range of the relevant venues. Bernard and Chrissy Farr would stay with the Wellinghams in Pimlico Road – Geoffrey and Sandy were invited. Alan's sister Maureen, nephew Sven and niece Susan would stay with him – his brother-in-law Harald could not spare the time to leave Sweden, just as Ian Thornton chose to keep the home fires burning in Kent. Celia's friends and colleagues from St Hugh's were invited to the reception, also Alan's colleagues from Carter Johnssen and a friend from his school days called William.

The wedding occurred five weeks after it was announced. Celia wore a cream-coloured dress, Alan a blue suit, and the witnesses numbered six. The reception was a lunch party, and the newly-weds motored off in the Minor to spend the honeymoon of a week in a small hotel in St Ives.

They were living together, which was different. The news that she was bearing her husband's child was the cause of quiet rejoicing. Celia loved Alan no less for learning more about him, and he seemed to love her likewise. He was a tender-hearted man, amenable, and patient. He was an unquestioning Christian and a true blue conservative. He had not married May until he was nearly forty – he had been a bachelor for long enough to become set in his ways; yet he tried to fit in with a second wife's habits and indulge her whims. Her pregnancy was somewhat restrictive sexually, but she was still willing and he was unfailingly able.

They naturally discussed the bread and butter

of family happiness. He was unambitious, would never be rich, but earned a good salary. Their joint earnings were more than the 'sufficiency' referred to by Victorians. However, if and when a child or children arrived, she would not work, would not be paid, and might need professional assistance. She deduced that they would keep their heads above water so long as he was fit enough to hold down his job; and the financial picture grew rosier in relation to the growth and independence of their children and her freedom to return to nursing. In a longer view of their finances, she would inherit Thanet Steps and he would no longer have to support his mother.

She did not worry Alan with quite such an onerous view of his responsibilities. He was dutiful and competent, yet he summoned from her a protective response. She noticed that, although he had become her guardian and shield, she did more of the guarding and shielding – they had started like that in St Hugh's, when she comforted him on account of May, and the pattern began to be repeated. She raised no objection: she had been dominated by Owen, and ended by divorcing him.

They were fully agreed on the marital home. They would sell his and her flats, and buy a house in a convenient position with a garden. And they would not buy a house in haste, after being so careful not to run the risk of regretting their marriage at leisure.

They met whenever they could, and he stayed in her flat if possible. Celia escaped the ills that pregnancy is heir to as a rule, a first pregnancy in particular, and especially so in the case of a woman of thirty. She felt better than usual, not worse. She had more energy and her spirits were higher. The Sturridges' times together were largely spent in walking round Highgate and its environs, house-hunting. They hunted by day at weekends and often at night midweek, stealing views of lit front rooms where families were eating a meal, peeping into bedrooms and imagining the scenes in progress behind net curtains. Their roaming was romantic: they invented the lives they might live, for example in a house with a front garden and a built-in barbecue, or again in a terrace house where they would cultivate wonderful window-boxes, or yet again in a flat with a south-facing balcony which would require an awning against the summer sun. They hoped for a back garden, a child-proof space, where their little offspring in the singular or plural could safely play. They linked the house they were looking for with their love – they would be destined to live in that house, just as they had been destined for each other, and sooner or later they would recognise it or it would recognise them, rather as their marriage seemed to them to have been written in the book of fate. She would explain her fitness for long walks through residential areas, and her inexhaustibility, by comparing herself with birds that tirelessly build complicated nests.

At last, after several false trails had led them nowhere, they found a little house and loved it at first sight. It was detached in a road of semi-detached houses built in an Edwardian seaside style. It must have been an afterthought, erected on a piece of ground not available until the rest of the housing development was complete. It had a porch with balcony above, a front door with stained glass inset, one ground floor window, two on the first floor, and a dormer. It had patches of garden back and front, a carport at one side, faced south-west and north-east at rear, was called The Homestead, and stood in Strawberry Road not far from Highgate's shops and transport facilities. Inside it had parlour, dining-room, two bedrooms, an attic, a bathroom and downstairs lavatory. It had belonged to two house-proud sisters, who had died and surely gained admission to heaven for leaving their Homestead so clean and smelling so sweet.

Celia and Alan sold their flats and bought it with the aid of a small mortgage. They were pleased to buy a double bed, and moved in with their furniture when Celia was seven months gone. Transplantation acted like a tonic. They were soon settled and comfortable. Problems were solved. Shopping was less of a strain than ever before for each of them, and buses and the tube took Celia within easy reach of St Hugh's if Alan was unavailable to drive her. She devoted her free time to preparing for the advent of the baby, while Alan hung pictures by Beatrix Potter in the second bedroom or so-called nursery, and created a garden suitable for a toddler.

Three weeks before Celia was due she said

goodbye to St Hugh's, or, as her colleagues preferred to put it, 'See you later'. Coincidentally, Dot called for an urgent meeting of the threesome. She and Con came to stay for a couple of nights at The Homestead, Dot sleeping in the nursery, Con dossing down on a camp bed in the attic.

The urgency of this reunion was owing to Dot's love-life. She was half-engaged to marry Jason Tyler, a writer, an Adonis, adorable, two years younger than she was, an awkward customer and a hypochondriac.

When Celia's friends had admired The Homestead, questioned her about her pregnancy and commented on her figure, they tackled the subject uppermost in all three minds.

What did half-engaged mean, what about the other 'half', was he financially solvent, and should they have read his books?

'He hasn't published a book yet,' Dot confessed. 'And he's only written two so far.'

'Are they good?'

'I think they are, I'm sure they are and he'll be one of the best writers, but he's rather stuck at present, poor love. Our story's a bit like him, a bit of a muddle at present. That's partly why I'm here.'

Would she tell her story?

She did so with a mixture of excitement and bewilderment.

'I met Jason at a weird party thrown by two antique dealers I've known for years – we sometimes buy their stuff and vice versa. They're Bohemians with an extra big B. The party was

122

for all sorts. I went in alone and came out with Jason. I was sliding away after ten minutes in the crush, almost in the dark, and he caught hold of me and asked where I was going. When I said, 'Out,' he said, 'I'll keep you company.' He took me to a pub and told me how miserable he was. He said he was a genius who wasn't recognised, a writer who couldn't write, a lover of women without a woman, and had no home to speak of – he actually had a room in the basement flat of a friend. Well – it's embarrassing – but there it is – I took him back to my place.'

Celia and Con were startled: they said they had always thought Dot was the sensible one.

There was laughter.

Dot resumed defensively: 'We had an amazing night. Jason's a genius in bed, I can vouch for that. And he's a sweet person, and clever, when he isn't dragging himself and everyone else down with his cares and complexes. He's stayed with me off and on since that first night. He disappears and then turns up – talk of wandering knights, at least he's a wanderer! The result is that he's more or less commandeered my private life, not that I mind much. But now he's determined to marry me.'

Celia and Con could not stifle exclamations of concern.

''To be or not to be is my question, too,' Dot said. 'Jason might become famous, and I'd feel a fool for having spurned him. He'd be an amusing husband, and I'd rather be the wife of a handful than a doormat. He presents enough

123

problems to keep me busy. On the other hand, although he loves children, I wouldn't want mine to be subjected to his black moods. What do you two think?'

Con asked: 'Is he a gentleman?'

Dot laughed and replied: 'He speaks proper, but he doesn't abide by any rules except his own, even if his parents are pillars of society somewhere up north. I believe his heart's in the right place.'

Celia asked: 'Has Sandy met him, has your father?'

'They have, briefly,' Dot replied. 'Their reactions have been so discreet I could slap them. Mother won't say a word against Jason, and Father simply coughs when he hears Jason's name. They're leaving the decision to me.'

And what was it, the others queried.

'I could marry him. I'm in love with him, I suppose. I could afford him. There are two little problems. The first but is that I don't dare. The second is that I can't refuse to marry him, because I'm afraid he'd throw himself out of my window if I did.'

Which problem carried more weight?

'Probably the second one,' Dot answered, and began to cry.

Celia and Con lent their shoulders to cry on. They consoled and comforted. They discussed Dot's dilemma for hours. Nothing was decided, yet a conclusion was reached. It was Dot's, it was feminine, and involved Jason as little as possible. She would cease to use birth control.

Celia's uncontrolled pregnancy was also coming

to a conclusion. The last three weeks went by. At the appointed time she felt a motherly pang and Alan drove her to St Hugh's. After a shortish labour she gave birth to a girl, a healthy baby, named Charlotte. Mother and child soon returned to The Homestead, and the three members of the family were happily reunited.

Celia had proved she was strong physically as well as morally; but her response to childbirth and to the success of her second marriage was humble thanksgiving. And gratitude to Alan meant that she wished to reward him. Consequently, three months after Charlotte was born she found she was again pregnant.

The same applied to Dot, who agreed to marry Jason Tyler round about now.

Celia's second child was a boy, a beautiful boy called Anthony, who perhaps inspired her to have yet another, Paul. In the course of her protracted labour to bring Paul into the world, something went wrong internally and put a stop to further procreation. She could not be sorry. She felt that her cup of good fortune was full, even to overflowing.

There was a church at the end of Strawberry Road, round the corner in Alyson Road. Celia passed it on the way to and from the shops. Sometimes the door of the church was open, and occasionally she would wheel her pram in and sit in a pew at the back for a few minutes. She was praising God, and resting her legs. She

125

was exhausted, of course, but never short of the energy needed to tend her babies, and never disheartened.

Life in The Homestead was like an advertisement for marriage, or a definition of contentment, but Celia would not have gone in for such a fanciful description. Alan ventured to speak of their peaceful days in terms more glowing than he was accustomed to use. As parents, both survived the interrupted nights, the dramas and the fluctuating emotions of their children, and looked sleek even as they yawned and nodded off in the middle of a meal or did the non-stop dirty work.

Official breakfast time was seven-thirty. It was comical and tragical. Alan left to catch a bus to his office in Stanmore at eight: the second-hand Rover that now replaced the Minor remained in the carport in case Celia should need it to drive a child to hospital. She attended to one infant, then two, then three: who played in the playpen in the nursery, or slept in a cot or a pram, while she washed and ironed, hung more washing on clothes lines, cleaned the house and prepared food. After the midday meal, during the afternoon, her brood was buckled into an ever larger pram, an eventual pram for three, and wheeled out for a walk – her walk – and into the shops. Tea was exciting, as was Daddy's return between six and seven. Bath-time was always fun and games, and bed-time was a treat for the parents. Alan and Celia loved to see the children asleep, those carefree faces, those pictures of innocence. Repeatedly, in the evenings, one or other or both would tiptoe upstairs to check that all was as they had always hoped it would be.

Celia tried hard not to show Charlotte that she favoured her new baby, Anthony. But Charlotte, although she had been a late developer and charmless, was turning into a stout independent personage in her second year, whereas Anthony was quiet and wistful, moreover a boy: the fact that Celia was not altogether successful in caring equally for the two, she ascribed to his sex as well as to his strange charm. Anthony was an ideal specimen of male infancy. He was pale-skinned with curly brown hair. He had one fault, he was apt to snuffle when he breathed. Celia showed him to an ear, nose and throat specialist, Dr Robinson-Whitehead, who operated at St Hugh's. Dr R W, as he was known to staff at the hospital, diagnosed adenoids, which he could whip out in no time at all – and the anaesthetic would not be a cause for concern.

Celia was nonetheless concerned. Anthony was a year old, too young for the knife, too sensitive to be rendered unconscious. She agreed with Alan that Dr R W was medically right, but claimed that her woman's intuition could not rid itself of suspicions. She shrank from the idea of an operation on Anthony of all little people. Yet she had to admit that he was not exactly flourishing, and might be held back by the congested breathing. She also knew that human physiology had a weakness for making mountains out of molehills, or, more realistically, for letting a snuffle develop into a proneness to pneumonia.

127

In the end she consented. She sat holding Anthony's hand throughout the operation in the theatre at St Hugh's, and sat by his bed in the hospital for twenty-four hours of recuperation. At home she gave him as much attention as she could spare, although he seemed well, breathing better than before. The improvement in his breathing continued, and Celia devoted more time to Charlotte – to Alan, too.

A few months later she was pregnant with Paul, and six months after that, when Charlotte was getting on for three and Anthony for two, it came to her notice that Anthony had not started to talk. He made moaning noises and pointed, but had not formed words, had not had to, since Charlotte was inclined to speak for him: 'Anthony wants cake … Anthony's wet his trousers.' Celia rang Con, who said her 'old' Jake had been a slowcoach and could only ask for food when he was two. Con had heard of other children beginning at three, and advised Celia not to fret. But Celia asked other people. Dot, by now the mother of Adam Tyler and deep into motherhood, endorsed Con's opinion. Alan's sister recommended a canary in the nursery – its song would rouse Anthony to join in; and a liberal friend had a psychotherapist she swore by.

Nobody panicked. Celia bought the canary and called it Timmy: unfortunately Timmy was not much of a songster. Anthony was growing satisfactorily in size, and seemed to be none the worse for being wordless. He was a very active child, and surely had an intelligence to match.

Paul differed from the other two, he was jollier. He laughed at life and put Charlotte and Anthony in the shade socially. But what a darling trio they were! Alan and Celia could not disguise the fact that they were proud of their eldest, who had learnt to read with her father's help, of Anthony whose dreamy blue eyes had a poetic quality, and of Paul who was already popular with everybody and should go far in the wider world.

Double trouble, even treble trouble, was an unbargained-for blot on the landscape. It was a mystery in a house where all was open and above board. Paul was found to have a sort of bruise on the side of his neck. It looked like a bruise, but was not tender. Celia spotted it one morning, the morning after a disturbed night – Charlotte was suffering from earache and had woken everybody with her cries of pain. Celia had eventually taken Charlotte into the double bed she and Alan shared, and Alan had gone up to the attic room.

Charlotte needed to see the family's doctor, Dr Railton, and Alan took her to the surgery in Alyson Road before going to work. Dr Railton or one of the other doctors in the practice would at least prescribe a suitable painkiller. Celia waved the Rover out into Strawberry Road, and returned to attend to Anthony and Paul. Upstairs in the nursery she re-examined the purplish mark on Paul's neck and arrived at a conclusion that was hard to credit. It reminded her of a game she had played at school – there had been a craze for it – the girls had given one another 'French burns', which was their name for applying oral suction to flesh and thus bringing blood to the skin and causing the semblance of a bruise. The practice was not sexual, and was harmless.

But how could Paul aged eleven months have received a French burn?

Possibilities now occurred to Celia. She noticed, or noticed that she had noticed in the night, that a chair had been moved in the nursery. A hard chair, her nursing chair, had been shifted not far, but closer to the cot in which Paul slept; and Paul was a supreme sleeper, slept sounder than any log, and only occupied about a third of the mattress within the cot. Someone, some little person, could have climbed on to the chair, over the side of the cot, in beside Paul and given the baby's neck a kiss amounting to a suck that was sufficient to summon blood to the surface of his skin. If Celia was right, astonishingly right, although she began to believe that the astonishment would be equal if she was wrong, the culprit, the sucker, could only have been Anthony, for Charlotte in the relevant period of time was either being cosseted on her mother's knee or sharing her mother's bed.

As possibility merged with probability, astonishment took a serious turn. For Anthony to have done such a thing was worse than strange. Why should one boy steal into the cot of another to perform a physically damaging action? That the answer was love, brotherly love, was incredible: Anthony was the opposite of demonstrative, and had actually been rebuked for pushing and pulling

Paul in a rough manner. That Anthony's motive was sinister was a Pandora's Box which Celia shied away from opening. Yet she could not duck a sudden flash of fear – she rushed to make sure the burn was on the left side of the neck, not the side of the jugular vein – if the skin over the jugular had been burned, the consequences were unthinkable.

She censored her horrible deductions. She was determined to assume that Anthony had meant no harm. The most pressing of her immediate problems was how to deal with him. She felt she must do so while Alan and Charlotte were out of the house – Alan might frighten the boy and Charlotte would be spiteful. The three of them, Anthony, Paul and herself, were together in the nursery: she called him by name.

Anthony's lack of response was another worry, although typical. He regarded her as if sightlessly and with no discernible expression on his perfect young face.

Celia carried Paul across to where Anthony knelt on the floor, knelt down beside him, and showed him the mark on Paul's neck.

'Look at this, Anthony! Poor Paul's been hurt. Do you see? Did you kiss him there?'

Anthony's reaction was almost nil. He did not look, let alone speak. He just slapped his thighs, a familiar gesture of his.

'Darling Anthony, won't you say something to me? I don't want you to kiss Paul so hard. I don't want Paul to be hurt. It was you, wasn't it? Can you hear me?'

He uttered a moan with a louder squeal at the end.

'I love you, Anthony, I love you and Paul and Charlotte. We must live happily and not hurt one another – no more kisses that make red marks.'

She kissed him: he was like a statue. She enfolded him in her arms and he at last raised his arms and put them round her neck, moaning and squealing louder still.

'It's all right, darling, all forgiven and forgotten. I'll have to get up and look after your brother. Let go, Anthony!'

He half released her, and she loosened his grip.

She shooed the cloud off, but it refused to disappear. She had become what she had always hoped never to be, a woman with secrets. She did not tell Alan what she suspected and what had happened between herself and Anthony: she told her husband and her first-born that Paul had somehow succeeded in bruising himself. Her new fears were unformulated, she could not contemplate them, and was far from ready to discuss them with any of the people who believed her golden bowl had no flaw, or to seek medical advice.

The situation returned to what had seemed to be normal. The Sturridges went to spend a weekend at Thanet Steps, where Celia again had trouble.

On the Saturday morning Alan took Charlotte to the seaside, Chrissy claimed a granny's right to stay with Paul, and Bernard drove Celia and

Anthony to a local beauty spot, a stretch of ancient woodland. Father and daughter were walking and talking, they were happy to be together, especially in their beloved Wild Wood. Anthony disappeared. He had been toddling along behind Celia, and was nowhere to be seen. She turned round and called him. She spotted the red bobble of the tam-o'-shanter he was wearing, it protruded from behind a tree off the path. She called again, his face appeared, their eyes met, and instead of stepping forward, back on to the path, he vanished, moved deeper in amongst the trees.

She ran the fifteen or twenty metres to where she had last seen him. He was not there. She plunged into the wood, calling even louder. The branches of the trees scratched her face. Again she saw him, peeping at her from behind a tree, not laughing or joking, not far away but on the other side of a bramble bush.

'Anthony, please come here, don't run away!' she ordered and begged.

He disobeyed. He withdrew out of sight. She scrambled round the brambles, but again he was not where he had been.

'Anthony, Anthony,' she called.

He was in the open, had reappeared but not where she had expected, and close enough for her to snatch him up. He was calm, she was panting and nearly crying and had lost her bearings. She now had to call to her father, who answered back, and at last they were reunited on the path.

Her father said to the boy: 'You're a monkey, you've led your mum a merry dance.'

Celia did not dispute this interpretation of the episode. She merely remarked with a mixture of admiration and exasperation that Anthony was awfully good at hide-and-seek. She had not the heart to try to explain why the dance was the opposite of merry. She said it was time to take Anthony home.

All the children had to rest or at least not to get too tired, for Con and her two were coming to tea. The visitors arrived at four o'clock. Con was her normal smiling self, Jessie was a heavy-boned five-year-old in glasses, and Jake a sturdy little man of four. A large meal had been prepared and was slowly consumed by the five children. After tea it was musical chairs, with Chrissy playing the piano and Bernard, Celia and Con joining in. At nearly the end of the game, when only Bernard and Jessie were competing, a shriek from a corner of the room stopped everything dead. Jake was hurt, his nose was injured, he covered it with his hand, between the fingers of which blood oozed. Con rushed to pick him up, Celia and the others crowded round. Jake was blubbering: 'He hit me, he hit me.' Anthony had done it – she was half-expecting the third disaster of a set of three. She jumped to the conclusion that he had hit Jake before Jake pointed the finger at him. Nobody had actually witnessed the blow; but the story was that Jake had been watching the two final competitors for the one remaining chair, and Anthony had approached him and for no known reason taken a swing at his nose.

The party ended miserably for Celia. She was not only sorry for Jake, insufficiently apologetic to Con because she could not explain Anthony's action and in truth did not understand it, and similarly embarrassed with regard to her parents and even Alan; she was also deeply worried by a brief exchange with Con while they were kissing each other goodbye.

'Darling Celia,' Con had said in an undertone, 'Could we meet for a minute tomorrow morning? I long for a quiet word – it's pretty urgent.'

Celia had agreed. Con would drive to Thanet Steps at ten. That the 'word' would be about Anthony, Celia had had no doubt. What was she to say? How much should she say?

Yet another nasty experience occurred during Saturday night and early on Sunday morning. The sleeping arrangements for the Sturridges at 42 Thanet Steps were complex, since five of them had to fit into the spare room and the attic. Celia divided them up for safety's sake. Alan would share the attic with Charlotte on a lilo and Paul on a futon, and Anthony would have one of the twin beds in the spare room and Celia the other. The children were in bed and asleep before the grown-ups had supper. Celia did not stay downstairs for long, she pleaded a headache and retired. She had locked the door of the spare bedroom in case Anthony took it into his head to stray, and she did not want Alan or her parents to notice. When she unlocked the door she was relieved to see that Anthony had not moved and was still sleeping. But at about midnight he woke and started to moan. She hushed him, took him to the lavatory, rocked him in her arms, kissed and shook him, forced him to swallow a baby-painkiller, all in vain. She told Alan she was coping and sent him back to bed. When her father investigated, she put Anthony's distress signals down to toothache or tummyache and said he would stop soon. At last he did stop, he stopped and slept, he and his mother slept together in her bed.

At breakfast on Sunday she apologised to everyone. Chrissy as usual misunderstood: she said Anthony was trying to talk and should be seeing a speech therapist. She said it was cruel that he was not talking – a dig at Celia.

Con rang her doorbell at ten. Alan said he would see to the children and Celia joined Con in Con's car – the weather was not good enough for a walk.

Con's concern was unexpected.

'You're looking so peaky,' she said. 'You worried me at the party yesterday. Can I help?'

Celia laughed and said: 'I thought you'd be worried by Anthony.'

'For hitting Jake? Jake's okay – children are beasts – every mother's hoping they'll grow out of being beastly. Are you worried about Anthony?'

'A bit. Yes, I am. I'm very worried.'

'Is it the talking?'

'That's the least of it.'

'What's worse?'

'It's too long a story.'

'You mustn't make yourself ill. Are you eating properly?'

'Quite right, Con – I'll try to make myself healthy and capable.'

'Would you like to come and stay with me? You could bring Anthony – we'd look after him together.'

'Thank you, Con. You're a brick. But I can't – I can't do much except worry at present – and I'll have to go in now – Alan's with Anthony and Alan knows nothing yet. Listen, listen – I want to postpone our discussion, do you mind?'

'Be strong, darling Celia!'

'I will!'

The Sturridges were leaving Thanet Steps after lunch. Bernard and Celia managed to exchange only a few meaningful sentences before the goodbyes.

He said to her: 'You're worried, aren't you?'

'Yes,' she replied.

'Can you tell me?'

'In time.'

'If there's anything I can ever do, ask me, won't you?'

'Yes.'

'I could give you a little money, if it's needed.'

'Thanks, Dad. But nothing's certain yet.'

'No – it never is – that's the good news,' he remarked, smiling.

Peace reigned at The Homestead for a few days. But Anthony's symptoms had emerged so suddenly and in such quick succession that Celia lived fearfully, straining not to let Alan or the other children see anything was wrong. On the Saturday following the family's weekend at Broadstairs, in the afternoon, Alan took Charlotte and Paul out for a trundle in their chariot – Anthony had shown no interest and been left behind. Celia washed and ironed, she was either in the kitchen or the garden or the extension where the washing-machine stood, and Anthony was in the sitting-room. For the third or fourth time she interrupted her work to look in on him. She saw a dreadful sight.

The cage of Timmy the canary was on the floor. Its stand had fallen or been pulled over, seed was scattered everywhere. And Anthony was on the floor too, he was holding Timmy, and Timmy had lost feathers, Timmy was obviously dead. He looked at his mother innocently and without expression, and held out the corpse of Timmy – he had a spot or two of blood on his hands. She controlled a scream, swallowed the great lump in her throat, took the poor limp yellow bird, rushed with it into the lavatory and pulled the chain. She fetched a cloth and returned to the sitting-room and wiped Anthony's hands clean, then dragged him into the dining-room and shut him in. She carried the cage and its stand out of the room and into the extension, where she hid it under towels. She then lugged the hoover into the sitting-room and hoovered up all the seed, sand, pieces of cuttlefish. She had just finished removing evidence of the accident or whatever it was by the time Alan returned with the other children.

She met them at the door, smiling and asking if they had had a lovely expedition. When Charlotte had been unbuckled and Paul had been lifted out of the chariot, as Charlotte ran into the kitchen and while she held Paul in her arms, she said to Alan: 'Timmy's dead – I'm going to tell Charlotte he flew away – please back me up, Alan, I'll explain later.'

'Is it bad, my dear? You look as if something bad's happened.'

'Yes, it has, but it'll keep. I promise to tell you later.'

'Very well. Where's Anthony?'

'In the dining-room.'

'Has he been playing up again?'

'No, dearest, no – later!'

In due course, at tea, Charlotte took the news that Timmy had joined the other free-flying birds in her stride. She was not a sentimental child; and Paul was too young to notice Timmy's disappearace, and Anthony's feelings were unknown.

As it happened, between tea and dinner Alan had an appointment to meet a man who was trying to organise a North London cricket team. Celia, as soon as he had gone, seized her chance to ring Dot.

Dot answered the telephone, which was a stroke of unexpected luck. Dot's baby, Adam, preoccupied her, just as Celia had been preoccupied by motherhood. The friends had not spoken or seen each other for months.

Celia began without preamble: 'I need moral support. Can we all meet soon? But I need your support now – so sorry – I've only got a minute or two...'

'Heavens! What's happened?'

'Advise me, Dot! I've got to tell Alan something awful – it's about my Anthony – question is – do I tell him the whole truth or lie and break it to him gently?'

'Is Anthony in trouble?'

'Yes – I'll explain everything when we meet – tell me in principle what I should do!'

'Is Alan strong enough to bear bad news?'

'He survived May's death – but this is different – I don't know – that's why I'm asking you.'

'Honesty's the best policy.'

'Thank you, Dot. I can't go on.'

'Are you surviving?'

'Just about.'

The Sturridge children were in bed by the time Alan returned. He went upstairs to say good night to them, reported to Celia in the kitchen that they were all asleep, agreed to sit down at the kitchen table and pour two glasses of red wine. She sat and was ready to talk.

'Anthony's ill,' she began.

'Is he? How ill? Are you sure?'

'Yes, I'm sure, but he may have extra illnesses that I've never heard of.'

'What is it, my dear?'

'Autism – he's autistic – it's a modern disease – he would have been called not right in the head or something worse not long ago.'

140

'But he's only slow to start speaking, isn't he?'

'No, Alan. Mysterious things have been happening. I didn't warn you because I hoped my suspicions were incorrect. He was probably born peculiar – I don't know – but there were no signs when he was a baby – at least none that I recognised. Since he's grown, recently, it's been one thing after another – and they're not mysteries any more. We'll have to take him to see doctors, I mean specialists.'

'Is the disease curable?'

'We'll find that out.'

'Do you mean it may not be curable?'

'I think, I'm afraid, not completely.'

'Oh no!'

'We'll take care of him.'

'How... Why...'

'We'll have the other two.'

'Wait, wait! Aren't you crossing bridges before we've come to them? What are these signs? I haven't seen them. What are the things you're talking about?'

'He has no words. His eyes are beautiful, but if you look in them you can see they're blank. He never laughs. His moans aren't attempts at communication, they're anguish. I saw a boy like Anthony at St Hugh's.'

'Is that all?'

'No. It's enough, but no. I believe he climbed into Paul's cot and gave him that blue bruise-mark on his neck – we used to do it to one another at school – you suck the blood into the skin – but Anthony might have injured Paul

141

badly – he must have wanted to.'

'That's hypothetical.'

'He was very bad at Thanet Steps. He lost himself in Wild Wood to torture me.'

'He's not as bad as that!'

'He hit Jake to hurt him. His moaning in the night was somehow to punish us – punish me – for removing him from our Homestead.'

'You're imagining it, Celia.'

'I'm afraid he killed Timmy.'

'Timmy? Why, what happened?'

Celia described the scene of the crime in the sitting-room before she had cleaned up the evidence.

Alan said: 'But Timmy might have died when the stand fell over and his cage hit the floor.'

'No – the latch on the door of the cage is supposed to be child-proof – the latch was somehow opened – Anthony's fingers are bruised – he must have reached in to catch the bird because his arm's scratched – and Timmy was partly plucked.'

'What did you do with Timmy?'

'I flushed him down the lav.'

'Celia...'

'Yes, dearest – are you all right? What's wrong with you? Alan!'

Alan had turned green in colour and seemed on the point of fainting. She stood up and cradled his head in her arms. He hiccupped and yawned and seemed to be slightly better. He apologised and cleared his throat.

'It's very feeble of me,' he said, 'but for a

moment I felt I simply couldn't go through another tragedy.'

'I do understand.'

'Of course we'll see it through together.'

'You must carry on with your life. We must keep cheerful. And I won't cross bridges prematurely. Now, let's have something to eat. I've got sausages and bubble and squeak in the oven.'

'I'm not very hungry.'

'No, nor am I – but you can drink more wine, and we'll try to nourish ourselves.'

'You're so brave,' he said.

'Appearances can be deceptive,' she replied.

They did drink a little more and did eat a bit. Then Celia spoke of bed-time. When Alan protested that it was early, she confessed that she was anxious in case Anthony woke and did damage. He made a gloomy grimace and wished that he instead of Anthony was to sleep with her in the double bed. She had to explain that she felt obliged to keep a close watch on Anthony.

'I can't let him be with the other children in the nursery – without supervision, that is. I'll devise a method soon of keeping Anthony under control. These awful discoveries – I've only looked at the opposite of the bright side today. I'm sorry to have distressed you, darling Alan. I'm sorry to have borne you an unhealthy son.'

'Not your fault, my dear, more likely mine – and as you say we must count our blessings.'

They agreed. They hugged and patted each other. She went upstairs – Anthony was still asleep – and in time she closed the bedroom door, drew aside the curtains and sat on the stool by her dressing table. Tears flooded into her eyes and cascaded on to her nightdress. She bent over from the waist, sobbing as quietly as she could and retching. The moonlight shone through the windows on her doubled-up figure shaking with surges of sorrow.

Three weeks elapsed before Celia, Dot and Con could meet again.

Meanwhile life at The Homestead continued naturally on the surface and far from naturally underneath. Alan still worked for Carter Johnssen in Stanmore. Celia kept house and looked after their children. Charlotte attended kindergarten, Paul learnt how to stand up. Anthony moaned and slapped his thighs. There was laughter, although Anthony did not join in. There were games for everyone except Anthony. The married couple did not share the marital bed – Anthony slept for parts of each night in Alan's place, and tired his mother by waking her with his moans and restlessness. He was averse to being comforted or cuddled. He was impervious to risk and apparently to pain: one day he jumped down about twenty stairs and fell like a sack of coal on the tiled floor of the hall, evidently spraining an ankle and hurting a shoulder, but he did not cry – and Celia did not dare to take him to a doctor for relatively minor injuries. Anthony was the ghost at the family feast. Anthony was the family's curse. Alan was depressed by him, but tried not to show it. Alan did not discuss Anthony with Celia. She was as steady as her unhappiness and bewilderment allowed her to be. She was obsessed – she and Anthony at least had obsessions in common. Hers was more straightforward than his: it boiled down to the question, what are we to do?

She read the entries about autism in medical dictionaries and encyclopaedias at the local library. The disease was only recognised in the 1940s. It was thought to be neurobiological – not a difficult diagnosis to arrive at. Treatment was experimental, which, in layman's language, meant practically non-existent.

She had friends at St Hugh's who might have had experience of her problem, but she was loath to spread the news of Anthony's illness, and was not ready to seek assistance from doctors.

Between the death of Timmy and her appointment to meet Dot and Con in Dot's new and larger flat in Pimlico, she could be glad that Anthony had done nothing positively bad.

They met at five in the afternoon. Alan was in charge at The Homestead, Ian Thornton was taking Jessie and Jake to tea with the Shelbys, Con's parents. Dot, first of all, had to introduce Adam to her friends – he was a handsome baby as babies go. Next she showed them round her flat. Jason Tyler was absent. He had rented a croft in the wilds of Scotland, where he hoped he would be able to create his masterpiece. He could not write at home – too distracting.

Apparently he did better on a cruise ship or in the cafés of Paris. But his hypochondria brought him back to Dot. She was humorous on the subject of his hypochondria and produced a fake menu card – she would produce it and ask him to choose either TB, VD or MS.

None of these preliminaries took very long. Celia was urged to spill the beans, and she repeated the story she had told Alan.

After they had been amazed, incredulous, appalled, compassionate and sorry, they wanted to know how he had taken it.

'I thought he was flaking out, he looked like fainting, but he recovered, and he's been supportive ever since.'

'Is that faint praise?' Dot queried.

'Alan's a fine man, I respect and love him, I love him best, but he was put through the wringer by the death of his first wife, he's said to me that he isn't sure he can stand another tragedy, and terrible illnesses are beyond his limits. He's being heroic, as I knew he would be and know he will be. The fact remains that he's one of my worries. I don't want to wreck his life. I don't want it to be wrecked. That's why I didn't tell him everything. There's something he might find altogether unacceptable.'

What was that?

Celia hedged: 'Anthony's so perfect in other ways. I'm not boasting when I say he's beautiful – I'm not a boaster. He has a look that makes my heart ache. It's difficult to think he's not perfect through and through, believe me! Alan could be terribly upset by the last chapter of the story to date.'

What did she mean?

'Anthony's got a malicious streak.'

'Haven't we all?' Con queried.

'I'm afraid he wanted to hurt Paul and your Jake, and cause me suffering in Wild Wood. I think he murdered Timmy deliberately.'

'Are you exaggerating by any chance?' Dot inquired.

Celia shook her head.

'Would I?' she said. 'I'd do the opposite if I could. We three have no secrets – and I'm sick of secrets. My worst worry is that Anthony's homicidal.'

The others would not have it, but Celia carried on.

'We're privileged, we've been healthy. I've nursed ill people, but I've been well, which was my protective barrier. Lack of privilege isn't poverty – being poor is often just an option. Lack of privilege applies to my Anthony and all those people who are very ill through no fault of their own. I'm finding myself in an underworld of horrors and terror. Honestly, Dot, I'm not exaggerating. Anthony will probably grow up, even to manhood. I've reason to expect him to treat someone as he treated Timmy – sooner or later he'll do it maliciously but without appreciating the criminal or sinful issues, with heartless innocence, with nothing in his eyes. What then? Which of us is most at risk? I'm guarding Charlotte and Paul, but that's another complication. Oh dear, I'm sorry.'

She cried.

The other two sympathised.

Con asked: 'Could I help you to look after him?'

Celia laughed through her tears.

'Darling Con, thank you, but no, I'm not going to drag you and yours into my battle.'

Dot asked: 'I could help with money, and I know my parents would, too. You'll have to have extra help with your family, all of them, not only Anthony.'

'Thank you, you're both so kind. Forgive me for whining, but it's such a relief to tell the unvarnished truth, it's such a treat. My list of worries in the order of their priorities is: Anthony, Charlotte and Paul, Alan, nursing and coping, my own health, assistance, money, housing – because if we have to isolate Anthony and employ somebody we'll need a bigger house. I haven't dared to calculate costs as yet, and I'm sure the same applies to Alan, whose profession is money – he's clinging to the hope of better news also for financial reasons. Dot, I will remember your offer, and I'm grateful beyond words, but I want to try to mind my business. The picture will become clearer, it must, it couldn't be more muddled. What next, or what comes first, what shall I go home and get on with?'

Dot and Con unified their answers: take Anthony to a specialist in his disease, steer clear of your local medical practice, seek advice at St Hugh's, do not involve Alan yet.

Yes, she said, she would do as she was told.

Then she said: 'I'm not giving Alan and Charlotte and Paul their dues. Anthony steals the love that should be theirs by rights. I can't let him do it. I always hated the prodigal son. Forget my grizzling, please – Anthony isn't prodigal – and I shouldn't feel as I sometimes do.'

It was natural, the others assured her, and inevitable.

At this point Adam Tyler weighed in with a yell, Dot attended to him, Celia insisted on talking of things other than herself, and soon she had to leave to travel back to her no longer homely Homestead.

The next day she obtained an urgent appointment with Mr Gibson, her gynaecologist and friend. She saw him one evening at St Hugh's, after Alan had returned from work and could be responsible for the children, and Mr Gibson had finished operating.

With apologies, she explained the urgency of her case. He was sorry to hear about Anthony, and warned her that doctors who specialised in autism were thin on the ground since they knew little, had access to no scientific knowledge, and were not sure how to ameliorate the effects of the condition. However, Dr Edward Speed ran a clinic and a residential home for autistic patients in a house not far from Highgate. It was near Muswell Hill, called Orchard Grange. Mr Gibson was willing to bypass the Sturridges' general practitioner for the sake of privacy and refer Anthony to Dr Speed.

A week later a letter for Celia from Dr Speed's

office arrived, suggesting a ten o'clock appointment for Anthony on a certain day, and that Mrs Sturridge might wish to plan to see work in progress at Orchard Grange afterwards – lunch would be available.

She brought Alan up to date with these developments.

'Could you manage the other children for most of that day?' she asked him. 'I don't know if I'll want to stay on, but I'd like to be able to if it was interesting.'

'Is this Orchard Grange reputable?' he replied.

'I imagine so – of course it is – Mr Gibson wouldn't have recommended a quack organisation – he said complimentary things about Dr Speed and that his clinic was a rarity.'

'I hope he won't put Anthony through a sequence of unpleasant tests.'

'So do I. There aren't any tests on offer, as I understand it. But Dr Speed must know a bit more than we do, and might prescribe useful pills.'

'Does Anthony need pills?'

'Oh Alan! He needs something we haven't given and can't give him. Please don't be stuffy about Dr Speed.'

'I'm sorry, my dear. I realise how anxious you are, as I am. I've asked around in the office and been told that autism's a tragic disease. But I've also heard of gradual recoveries, if not cures. Anthony was a pest at Broadstairs, I grant, but since then he hasn't been bad. I feel that in a happy family atmosphere he might well improve,

150

even grow into a fairly fit man – I'm sure the other children would teach him to talk in time. I merely beg you not to be hasty. I'm a great believer in letting sleeping dogs lie.'

'Alan, I'm so sorry to disillusion you, but I must, I love you too much to let you get a worse shock than the one I'm going to give you. Our home isn't happy any more, and we're under pressure to improve matters before we're all utterly miserable for years. I've no bright ideas, can't say how to bring about improvements, can only say I'm trying. Please support me! Now – what is certain is that Dr Speed's going to charge me money for Anthony's appointment – Mr Gibson didn't, but Dr Speed will and will live up to his name, I expect. Can I pay with our "household" cheque book?'

'Ah, yes – yes, my dear. I hope he'll earn his money.'

This conversation added to Celia's burden of anxiety. Alan had made a valid and disturbing point: Anthony had been good as well as silent for weeks. Had she exaggerated? Was she mistaken?

After breakfast on the morning of the appointment, Celia and Alan united to explain to Charlotte and Paul that Anthony had to see a doctor. They had agreed to make light of it. They announced the object of the exercise when Alan was carrying Anthony to the car. Charlotte was not particularly interested, and Paul showed no sign of comprehension.

Celia drove off with Anthony behind her. She talked to him cheerfully for part of the journey, although doubts gnawed at her. She resolved on no account to become too involved with Dr Speed. Anthony was loose in the back of the car – seat belts were not yet invented – but the rear doors and the front passenger door were secured by childproof locks. He clambered up and wedged a foot into the space between the front seats, apparently to see more through the windscreen. Then he reached forward and covered Celia's left eye with his hand. She told him not to, spoke sharply, and raised her hand from the steering wheel in order to remove his. She explained that he must not do a thing like that, and why. He did it again, the sequence was repeated, and yet again. She had to stop the car and give him a lecture.

They drove on. Anthony discovered a better way of driving them into the ditch. He stood on the edge of the back seat, leant on the back of the driver's seat, and, bridging across, put his arms round his mother's neck and covered one of her eyes with one of his hands. She shouted at him and released his hand. He clasped her neck with it and covered the other eye with his other hand. She was frightened, was driving all over the road and being honked at, and again stopped the car, this time in a dangerous position. She extracted Anthony from the back and plonked him on the front passenger seat, lectured him, and drove on, all in a rush.

His next act was to stand up on the seat, defying orders to sit still, and scramble on to her extended arms holding the steering wheel, and twist his body so that he was able to cover both her eyes with both his hands at the same time. She screamed at him and had to brake hard, swerved, expected to crash or be crashed into, but was lucky, was able to throw him off, pull into the side of the road, and turn off the engine.

Anthony sat beside her, showing no trace of emotion. He was so young, small, sweet – how could he be so dangerous? Celia's mind was changed. She leant across and hugged him.

'Oh my darling boy,' she crooned. 'I'm sorry for you and me and everything, sorry, sorry!' She pleaded with him to allow her to drive. She stifled an awful idea that he had taken steps to avoid being seen by Dr Speed. She started the car in a determined manner and drove very slowly forwards close to the verge.

They reached Orchard Grange late. She was exhausted and emotionally drained. She registered only that the house was large and welcoming. She held Anthony's hand firmly and led him in, and a pleasant person, middle-aged, not in uniform, one of several people bustling about in the hallway, said that her lateness was not a hanging matter and escorted her without delay along a passage and into a consulting room, where a youngish brisk dark-haired man stepped out from behind his desk, smiling, and extending his arms towards Anthony.

Dr Speed took Anthony into his arms, spoke his name – 'Hullo, Anthony, good morning, Anthony' – put him down and let him go. He then shook hands with Celia, indicated a chair for her to sit on, and returned to the chair behind his desk.

He was friendly, encouraging, friendly enough for her to tell him why she was late and the awfulness of it. He listened, he did not take notes. There were toys on the floor – Anthony was fingering some wooden bricks. The room was empty otherwise – the desk was not a big daunting one.

Dr Speed prompted her. She talked as she had not meant to. A tray of coffee for two and orange juice for Anthony was brought in by another pleasant lady. The atmosphere was soothing. The doctor seemed to have time to burn. Celia ended by entrusting him with her whole story. Anthony was intermittently restless; but Dr Speed pointed out that there was nothing for him to damage, the window was discreetly barred and the door opened and closed by secret means. Celia shivered, but appreciated the common sense of the arrangements.

When she had finished talking, he spoke.

'About myself,' he said, 'I'm a qualified doctor and psychiatrist, married with two children, a boy and a girl, and we live down the road. I practised medicine, then psychiatry for several years, and began to specialise in autism. An aunt of mine died and left me Orchard Grange, a farm with a hundred acres of land. Instead of selling it, I set up a home for autistic boys suffering from the more extreme manifestations of autism – autistic girls are rare, and I couldn't cope with mixing the sexes. The aims of the Orchard, as we call it, are twofold: to study the condition of autism, and to provide the boys with a safe haven and protect their families. At present, as constituted, we look after our patients through the years they would have been educated at schools. We don't charge fees, we survive – to date – thanks to government grants and charity. We have room for twenty-five patients up to the age of puberty, and ten patients between puberty and the age of twenty: the two classes of patients are separated. We have four female professional nurses here, two male nurses, domestic staff, and many volunteers, mostly the parents of the boys. I hope you aren't in a hurry today – spend the day and see for yourself how the Orchard works! It exists, I regret to say, for children whose symptoms are not mild. There would be room for Anthony if you thought we could help him and your family. Do you feel up to investigating further?'

Celia said yes. She was escorted back to the hallway – Dr Speed carried Anthony, who did not protest, and introduced them to a middle-aged lady in civilian clothes, Maggie by name. Dr Speed took his leave, saying he would see Mrs Sturridge later. Maggie unlocked a door into a large room, like a drawing room, which had linoleum on the floor and only coloured pouffes scattered round. Anthony threw himself on to the pouffes. Spring sunlight and pained cries entered through fully open french windows, and Anthony ran out into a garden area that was part park and part playground. Celia followed, but he was already involved with the children and their attendants in the vicinity of a climbing frame.

Celia stayed at Orchard Grange until six o'clock that evening. She kept an eye on Anthony, who appeared to be more at home in these surroundings than he was at The Homestead. She received non-stop information that made her head spin, and struggled to believe her eyes and ears. She talked further with Dr Speed, who, eventually, assured her that Anthony would not be noticeably sad and might even be content to spend the night in one of his dormitories with nursing staff in attendance.

She drove back to Highgate alone. At least she felt safer than when she was driving in the opposite direction. She was in time to give Charlotte and Paul their supper and put them to bed. She hugged and kissed them good night fervently.

She had hugged Alan too. Now, when they were on their own, she tried to give a fuller description of Orchard Grange and explain why she had decided to let Anthony stay there. She told him that money had not been mentioned. She said the place was inspiring.

'It may do Anthony good,' Alan conceded.

'That's my hope,' she replied.

'He'll be all the more pleased to come home,' Alan said.

She did not answer.

'Won't he?' he asked.

'He may not come home,' she replied.

156

PART THREE

Celia had regrets for saying what she had said, but no regrets for thinking it.

Alan was deeply shocked by her idea, and, it emerged, her plan to banish Anthony from The Homestead and consign him to Orchard Grange. The boy, the child had not been given a fair chance to recover from his illness – autistic children could sometimes recover, Alan had checked. That she, who was so maternal, and principled, was willing to chuck Anthony out, on to a sort of dungheap, because he was troublesome, passed his understanding. Moreover, she seemed to have arrived at this decision, which condemned her son to be a homeless outcast, in a matter of a few hours. What would become of him? What had become of her? He was afraid that something had affected her judgment. He felt he would never be able to agree to such a cruel solution of the problem of Anthony – and how were they to be sure that he would always be a problem?

Celia apologised for shocking him. She had only stated her opinion of what was in the best interests of Anthony, the other children, Alan himself, and her health, which would not be equal to the strain of caring for a chronically sick child as well as being a wife, housewife and responsible for Charlotte and Paul. The alternatives to boarding Anthony at Orchard Grange were horrid – perhaps Alan had not visualised the future with Anthony at home. She would need help. She would need at least a special sort of living-in-nanny who would help with the nights – Anthony could not be left to his own devices at night. They would need accommodation for Anthony separate from the other children and secure, and would therefore have to move into a bigger house. The more expenses were considered the more they mounted up, as Alan must realise.

The difficulties did not stop there, in fact they had scarcely begun. Alan did not know, had not as yet had to register, that their Anthony had a mischievous, spiteful, destructive and even malevolent streak – no, she was not saying so in order to justify Orchard Grange, she loved Anthony very much, she hated having to say his character was flawed, the whole business of reorganising his life and the family's life was breaking her heart. But facts were facts, and she had experience of them. Unhappily, she had had to accept that Anthony had intended to hurt his brother Paul, herself in Wild Wood, Jake Sturridge and Timmy the canary. She could agree that he had not been awkward for the weeks after Timmy's death, but today, in the car, driving him to Orchard Grange, he had done his damnedest to kill the two of them.

She described their battle in the car. When Alan suggested that Anthony was playing a game and had no conception of the dangers, Celia replied that such an assumption was too great a risk for her to run.

160

'You see, if he had administered the French burn to the other side of Paul's neck, he could have ended up like Dracula, sucking blood from Paul's jugular. I didn't oust you from our bed exclusively because I was worried about Anthony's health, it was because I was worried about the health of Charlotte and Paul if they were sleeping in a bedroom with Anthony. I thought Anthony – unsupervised – would injure or even somehow kill one of them.'

Alan protested. Celia allowed that she was taking an extreme hypothetical view, but said mothers had to expect and be ready for the worst even as they hoped for the best. She reverted to the episodes in the car: they had frightened her more than anything else, frightened and shattered her. On the way to Orchard Grange she had wondered if she was doing the right thing. After it she did not consider the possibility of turning back.

Time passed without their noticing as they talked. But Alan looked increasingly pale and tired, and Celia was overcome by the exhaustion of her alarming, topsy-turvy, and above all long day. They agreed that they were done in. He pulled her to her feet from the sofa where they had sat, and they held hands on the staircase up to the bedroom floor. They peeped in at their children, who slept safely, and retired to their double bed, where Alan fell asleep and Celia at length lost herself and all her tormenting pros and cons.

In the morning Celia was pleased that Charlotte

did not mention Anthony – Paul was oblivious.
After breakfast, while the children made mud
pies in the garden, she again tackled the subject
which, she sensed, Alan would have liked to
postpone or avoid.

'I'm going to see Anthony this afternoon,' she
began.

'Ah,' he commented.

'It's Saturday – I'll go this afternoon – will
you take care of Charlotte and Paul?'

'Yes, my dear.'

'Can you bear more explanations?'

'Of course – please do explain.'

'Orchard Grange is extraordinary. It's a lovely
house, and a lovely place, believe it or not. I
wouldn't have left Anthony there if I hadn't
thought so. Dr Edward Speed owns it and runs
it, he's a philanthropist and a scientist. The
patients are all boys, young ones and, in a separate
stream, some older ones up to the age of eighteen
or so. I only saw the young boys, about twenty-
five of them. They were in a big garden enclosed
by a wire fence – Anthony ran about with them.
The Orchard – that's what they call it – is a
registered charity. The parents of boys are expected
to contribute to the expenses – we'd have to pay
our bit, but parents also help out by volunteering
to do a lot of the donkey work. The government
gives grants, but the Orchard costs more than
what's granted. There are professional nurses and
other staff. Sorry if I'm sounding businesslike,
but I don't want to be irresponsible.'

'Thank you for clarifying some of the issues.

What might our monetary contribution amount to?'

'I'll find out. I understand that it wouldn't be beyond our means. I've taken another decision – don't flinch, darling – my decisions are taken partly to spare you – I'll return to work at St Hugh's. I could do two days of nursing and put Charlotte and Paul in the St Hugh's nursery. That would pay most of our contribution to the Orchard, and ... and I might be allowed to leave Charlotte and Paul in the nursery on the other two days I spend with Anthony. Alan, I can't lose touch with him, and my work with the other mothers would complete our contribution. I've already agreed to do four hours this afternoon. I'll be away from two until sixish. Will you manage?'

'Four hours!'

'Darling Alan, be realistic! Fathers turn to at the Orchard. I know you'd be ready to do your whack, but I won't let you – one broken heart is quite enough in our family. I'm a nurse, you're a solicitor – I'm used to grisly sights, you only come up against them on paper. Am I asking too much of you?'

'No – no – but I wonder if your project will be successful.'

'I trust Dr Speed. You could meet him, I'm sure you'd give him the benefit of the doubt. The nurses in charge of Anthony are trained to deal with autism, they're therapists and teachers. If he shows any improvement, and might be able to live in a normal environment, we can bring him home. Until then, until that perfect day, because of Dr Speed, we could give Charlotte and Paul an upbringing without shadows and fears. We might learn to be happy again if we thought Anthony was not more unhappy than he was born to be for some unknown reason. Anyway, we've got to try to forgive God for moving in such a mysterious way.'

'Indeed! Will you promise me something?'

'In theory, yes.'

'Will you promise to bring Anthony back today if there's any sign that he's homesick?'

'I will, I do.'

They left it at that.

She duly returned to The Homestead at six-fifteen on the Saturday afternoon. She had to feed Charlotte and Paul and then put them to bed. At last she and Alan were alone together.

'How was he?' Alan asked.

'Not bad, okay, very good really.'

'What do you mean?'

'He took no notice of me. He was vaguely interested in the other children, and he stood and moaned. He didn't acknowledge my existence.'

She cried then, at last, again, and could not be comforted; but she had proved to her own satisfaction that she had not done wrong, and Alan was more inclined to agree.

The next day, Sunday, also in the morning, she continued her conversation with Alan. She was looking in at Orchard Grange in the afternoon, just to make sure that Anthony was no worse.

She said: 'Whatever happens, whether or not

my plan can be worked out, it's going to be misunderstood and controversial. If people know, they'll criticise. I'll be called an unnatural mother, selfish, cruel, et cetera, and you'll be blamed for not having brought me to my senses or for colluding with me. Provided we mind our own business, they might mind theirs. Who needs to know, and what's our story?'

'Oh Celia,' he burst out, 'I can hardly bear to think of the untruthfulness, of you telling lies when you're such a truthful person – I love you for your honesty – and for that matter I hate to think of myself spinning a web of deceit!'

'No – well – I'm sorry – but our children come first, Charlotte and Paul, also Anthony's good name supposing he were to get better. I'm taking action for all our sakes, because we're trying to salvage the family. We can't spoil everything by broadcasting our news from the rooftops. Our plight isn't gossip. Let's put our heads together, Alan – we must be prepared.'

She persuaded him, she compelled him. She would tell her father, not her mother; Dot and Con – the three of them always swapped secrets and secrets were safe with them; and their GP, Dr Railton. He would not tell his mother, whose heart was weak and health failing, nor his sister Maureen, who was stuck in Stockholm and seldom communicated, but he would tell the relevant partner at Carter Johnssen, Andrew Brook, and a younger partner, Michael Ayres. Andrew could draw up new wills. He and Michael could be the Sturridges' executors, have power of attorney if required, and, most importantly, could be named as guardians of the children, Anthony in particular.

Otherwise, in answer to inquisitive questions about Anthony, Celia thought she and Alan could reply that he suffered from an allergic syndrome and had to spend time in hospitals both in England and abroad. She was dead against publicising the word 'autism' – ignorant people would think it meant 'mad'. She was aware that some of the other mothers at Orchard Grange could have wagging tongues, but surnames were not used, the identity of patients was protected, and discretion amounting to secrecy seemed to be a rule observed by everyone concerned.

Alan went along with all her suggestions.

A month elapsed.

The plan was working smoothly enough for Celia to take Charlotte and Paul to stay the night with her parents at Thanet Steps, leaving Alan in The Homestead in case he should be needed by Anthony – he was willing to act in such an emergency, although he had never been to Orchard Grange.

They arrived at supper-time, after Celia had done her day's work at St Hugh's.

'Where's Anthony?' Chrissy Farr immediately asked. 'Where's my beautiful Anthony?'

Celia said she would explain later, and took her time to put Charlotte and Paul to bed.

Downstairs, Chrissy broached the subject without delay.

'Where is he? What's the mystery?'

'He's not well, Mother. I'm afraid you won't be seeing him for a time. He's allergic to everything and has to be in a completely sterile atmosphere.'

'Good gracious, when did this come to light?'

'In the last few months – he's in a sort of sanatorium – he's all right – I see him regularly – and we hope for better things.'

Bernard Farr spoke up.

'I'm so sorry, my dear. What an awful discovery for you and Alan as well as for the boy, although he's probably too young to be much affected.'

'True, Dad – and the situation's just about under control. To tell the truth,' Celia gulped and continued, 'it's a sore spot, and I'd be grateful if we could avoid it while I'm here. Besides, Charlotte and Paul don't know what's happened to their brother, and Alan and I are determined not to involve them in his trouble.'

'I understand that,' Bernard answered. 'And we'll respect your wishes, won't we, Chrissy?'

Chrissy had to have a last word: 'Can't I just send my grandson a get-well card?'

'Send it to me, Mother,' Celia replied with a touch of asperity.

They had dinner, and retired to bed early. The next day in the morning, Celia engineered a short walk alone with her father, leaving the two children in the care of their grandmother.

'Dad,' she began as soon as they were out of the house, 'I've told you fibs. Anthony's not what I said he was last night, he's autistic, and I've put him in an institution to give the other children a chance to be happy while they're young.'

He stopped walking, looked at her hard and sadly, kissed her and said: 'You're the bravest of the brave, my dear.'

She begged him not to praise her – 'I'll break down if you're kind' – told him a potted version of the whole story – and said: 'You're almost the only person who knows it, Dad. This afternoon I'm meeting Con and Dot, and I'll tell all because they'd tell me if they were in my kind of boat. That's how private I want to keep it, not on account of shame or embarrassment, but for the sake of Charlotte and Paul, also Alan, who has to be spared as much as possible.'

'I promise never to betray your trust, Celia, and not to drop the slightest of hints to your mother.'

They laughed. She hugged him gratefully, and he voiced a query by means of the two words: 'Brass tacks?'

She had them at her fingertips, the amount of money Alan could provide for Orchard Grange, her earnings at St Hugh's, the fact that Alan's mother was old and ill and costing a lot of money, and the outside chance that Anthony might become fit to rejoin his family.

How had Celia managed to get away to Thanet Steps, Bernard asked, and why on a weekday instead of at a weekend?

'The weekends are for us to be with Charlotte and Paul,' she replied, 'and play together and try to have a laugh. Today is actually one of Anthony's days, but I've asked another mother to keep an eye on him.'

'I'm sorry we've robbed Anthony of your company.'

'Oh Dad! I can't have explained very well. You know roughly what autism is – everyone who knows only seems to know roughly – but the reality is different from knowing like that. Anthony won't notice that I'm not at Orchard Grange as usual, at least he'll show no sign of noticing. I can't guarantee that he ever recognises me, although I'd love to be persuaded that he does. When I go to Orchard Grange to be with him, he spends most of our time running away from me.'

'I see now,' Bernard commented.

A little later, turning back to number 42, he asked: 'How is Alan reacting to your predicament?'

'Gallantly, stoically, as you'd expect, but it's really more than his temperament and constitution could or should have to bear. I left your telephone number with Orchard Grange in case I had to be contacted.'

'Poor Alan! Has he been to see Anthony?'

'Oh no.'

'Could I come one day?'

'I don't want to answer your question, darling Dad.'

In the afternoon of that day Celia escaped to the house in the country where Con Thornton lived. Bernard and Chrissy were to watch over Charlotte and Paul's siesta. Dot had been summoned to the friends' meeting and had motored down with Adam Tyler. The three of them were soon drinking tea at Con's kitchen

169

table. They admired Adam, who had bawled himself to sleep. Con's two were visiting friends. Her husband Ian was looking at land and Dot's Jason had apparently found he could write best in an East End pub, and was relatively calm and contented.

'Where are your children?' Dot and Con asked Celia almost in unison.

At Thanet Steps, Celia replied; two were at Thanet Steps, she corrected herself; the third was not there – and that was why she had to talk to her friends.

She continued. Her answer was again Anthony's story, which she cut as short as she could. Dot and Con were saddened, and to some extent mystified.

Con had never heard of autism, and Dot had only a hazy idea of the illness.

Celia said it was new, its cause not fully understood, that it attacked children around the age of two and a half years, male children as a rule, and was incurable, although a small percentage of victims could throw it off.

Symptoms? Anthony was speechless, very withdrawn, introverted, had odd obsessive mannerisms, and could be unhappy. Celia then described the episodes that had driven her to take radical action, ending with his dangerous game in her car. She also mentioned his relentless moaning.

Celia said she had realised before she entered the Orchard that she could not cope with Anthony at home, that is at The Homestead as it was and as they had been living in it. The alternatives that were threatening her were either an impossible expenditure of money, or to let Anthony go into the sort of institution where people like him were controlled by sedation.

Dr Speed was an answer to her prayers. Orchard Grange was nothing like a tragic prison. Anthony in its garden, with the other ill boys, was neither worse nor better than he had been elsewhere. Truly, the main difference for him was that he had nurses and ten or twenty knowledgeable mothers looking after him all the time.

'I left him there overnight, and decided in the car driving home that the Orchard was the solution to our problems, his, Alan's, mine, and insured Charlotte and Paul's upbringing. It's not a life sentence for Anthony – we'll bring him home if or when we can. Sorry to talk so much, I had to tell you, I need support – God knows where we go from here!'

The support was forthcoming.

Then Dot asked: 'How old is Anthony now?'

'Getting on for four.'

'A toddler?'

'Yes, except that he never toddled clumsily – he was born quick on his feet.'

'He's very young.'

'How could I wait? I want the others not to remember him too clearly.'

'How old are the others? Remind me.'

'Charlotte's only eleven months older than Anthony, and she's young for her age. She's hardly mentioned him – I think he might have frightened her. Paul's one and a bit.'

Con had a question.

'What's Dr Speed like?'

'He's committed to his Orchards – there's another one opening in Scotland. His ideal is to relieve families of the strain of dealing with an autistic child, and at the same time to remove the child from a competitive environment, from comparisons with normal children, and provide professional care.'

'I meant, what's he like as a man?'

'He's in his forties, and extremely kind.'

'Is he attractive?'

All three of them laughed.

'He's admirable,' Celia replied, 'and I like him, but not in that way.'

They laughed again.

'Are you on Christian name terms?' Con persisted.

'Oh yes – he's Edward to everybody connected with the Orchard.'

Dot reverted to relevant matters.

'What happened when you took Anthony to meet Dr Speed? Was Anthony examined and tested?'

'Not at all – it was surprising – Anthony just meandered round the consulting room, and Edward talked to me for ten minutes. Of course he could diagnose Anthony's illness at a glance – anybody who knew anything could – and there are no worthwhile tests. Anthony and I spent that day at the Orchard, while Edward studied him. When I had to leave, he talked to me again. He said he could offer us a safe haven, no more.

172

I asked if Anthony could stay overnight, and he said yes. The next day Anthony was okay, and I virtually accepted Edward's offer on a permanent basis.'

'Before Alan was in the picture?'

'Alan wouldn't have decided and I felt I had to.'

'You persuaded him?'

'Sort of.'

'Does he agree with you now?'

'With reservations – he's so kind-hearted, and he counts the cost.'

Con said: 'The money must be another problem.'

'We're managing. The Orchard office people make allowances if I'm late with my contribution.'

Dot and Con summed up by praising her realism, resourcefulness, maternal devotion, and heroic readiness to slave away to pay the bills.

Celia was reduced to tears.

They embraced her, and pressed her to have a fresh cup of tea.

'You don't understand,' she sobbed.

What did they not understand?

'My responsibility...'

She could not finish the sentence. But she dried her eyes, and was eventually able to resume.

'Everything bad that Anthony seemed to do could have been misinterpreted, and I'm haunted by imagining that Timmy died a natural death and Anthony only covered my eyes in the car for a joke. What have I done to him? He may just be retarded, and would have learned to speak if I had given him time. He might not have more than a touch of autism. By locking him in with all those really autistic children I'm afraid I've violated his soul and robbed him of his chance to cure himself. I've been fearfully bossy, yet I can't retract my bossiness. I feel more like a villain than a heroine, and there's no help for it or for me, and there it is.'

Alan Sturridge was badly hurt by the whole autism issue. He was a decent man, a law-abiding citizen, self-respecting and modestly proud of his record of filial duty, of having honoured his parents, done well at school, served in the army, qualified as a solicitor, held down a demanding job, paid his taxes and even gone to church occasionally. He could not adjust to having been singled out for two of the harsher sentences of fate. To have had to nurse his first wife into a premature grave seemed to have exhausted his powers of resistance to the visitation of cruel illness on his elder son. He did not grumble, he was stoical on the surface, but he felt he was being victimised, unfairly ill-used, and powerless.

Celia sensed it. She had married Alan knowing that he was less forceful than she was; but he was encouraged by her forcefulness and sexual warmth. He was man enough for her after the selfish masculinity of Owen Pennant. There had been trust in their marriage. They agreed to buy The Homestead, and he had not objected to her three pregnancies. Their happiness was not shadowy – they had both been unhappy and were grateful to have emerged into the sunlight. The misdeeds of Anthony, as she saw them and described them to Alan, were a fork in their road.

They travelled in gradually diverging directions. He could not quite go along with her dramatic interpretations of Anthony's behaviour. He resisted Celia's suspicions, he preferred to sweep them into a legally unproven void. He shied away from autism. He realised Anthony was not well, or normal, or like his other children, but took a wait-and-see line. And he countered her despair with his tranquillising truisms, which were apt to reduce her to grinding her teeth.

Sex is the tell-tale of matrimony. They were tired by parenthood, they were preoccupied by Anthony, and for a few months they exclusively slept in their double bed. But as soon as Celia faced the fact that Alan was not entirely of her mind, not convinced that Anthony was so ill as she believed he was, she sought reassurance in the feminine manner. He could not always provide it.

Orchard Grange exacerbated the marital problem. Alan did his bit with money, and more than his bit when his mother died and ceased to be a drain on his resources; but on one occasion he described the Orchard as a 'waste-bin for children', and on another he called Edward Speed a 'conman'. The new tension between the Sturridges had an inflammatory effect on her libido and the effect of cold water on his. She

175

was frustrated, he was embarrassed; and both were annoyed that their personal relationship interfered with their feelings for their poor little boy.

Later, perhaps a year after Anthony's admission to the Orchard, Celia missed a monthly period and jumped to the conclusion that she was in for the change of life. It fanned the flames of desire, and he could not put them out. Their happiness was turning into sadness. They could operate separately and efficiently, but no longer as the team they once were.

Round about this time Alan's conscience-stricken regret for not having visited Anthony provoked Celia to call his bluff: she might not have done so if they had still been close.

'Come with me,' she said one morning, on a weekday on which he was working at home rather than in the office, as she was setting off for the Orchard.

It was a challenge – she had previously discouraged him from seeing Anthony.

He climbed into the car, he was not a coward. They dropped Charlotte and Paul at school and nursery, and drove on more or less in silence. Before they reached their destination she issued warnings.

They found Anthony in the garden with the other children. He took no notice of their summons, ignored his father, shrugged off physical contact and ran away, moaning. Alan looked ten years older than his fifty-two years – he had not believed it would be so bad as she had warned.

She took him to the staff room, fetched him a mug of tea, urged him to go for a drive or have a long walk in the countryside, and left him in order to attend to her duties.

They met as arranged at one o'clock for a sandwich lunch and more tea, and at four she escorted Alan to Edward Speed's consulting room. She introduced the two men nervously – she had fixed the appointment, and knew Alan had questions to ask.

She was glad he did not want to probe into Anthony's lavatorial difficulties; but his first proper question was worse for her in that it related to her reasons for committing Anthony to an institution.

He wished to know if his son had recently shown any violent tendencies.

Edward Speed said no, nothing to worry about, and explained that children of his type were more inclined to hurt themselves than anyone else, since they were unrestrained by risk.

Alan's second and last question referred to Celia's bad experience in the car: had Anthony deliberately tried to blind her and cause an accident?

'I can't say, autistic motivation is still a closed book,' Edward replied.

'Could he have known it was dangerous to cover the eyes of a driver?'

'Possibly.'

'Could he have been playing?'

'Autistic children don't exactly play. Those in my care could be vicious if they were not watched over. They're so pent up within themselves that they need to use any safety-valve, vocal or physical. Whether or not they foresee consequences is another matter.'

Alan left it at that. He had made the point that Anthony might not be precociously homicidal: which consoled him, put Celia in the wrong and made her angry with herself for having allowed him anywhere near the Orchard. In the car going home he aired his opinion that Anthony was obviously deep in his disease for the time being.

He also said: 'I do see that in his present state he would exert an oppressive influence at home,' and she had to bite her lip in order not to retort, 'Stale buns!'

Alan did not return to the Orchard. He slightly compensated for not suggesting another visit by heaping praises on Celia's conscientiousness and energy – the slightness was the measure of his overlooking her love of Anthony.

In another year her father stayed at The Homestead. He drove over one evening and left about twelve hours later – it was like a secret assignation. He had not seen his grandchildren for ages – Celia had not dared to expose them to an inevitable interrogation by her mother. Now Chrissy was in hospital, she had had her gall-bladder removed and was doing well enough drowsily after the operation for Bernard to sneak away. He and Celia commiserated with each other over their lies; but he insisted that they were lying in a good cause, not to make mischief.

178

In the morning after his arrival he had breakfast with Charlotte and Paul and walked them along to school. Then, as promised, Celia and he drove in separate cars to the Orchard – he would drive on to Thanet Steps. He was upset by meeting, or rather seeing in the distance, Anthony. He was sorry for all the 'lost' boys, and especially for Anthony's mother, his daughter. Yet his afterthoughts were almost as distressing as Alan's had been. He said that if he should ever be a widower, alone, he would like to remove Anthony from the Orchard and care for him at Thanet Steps. The implications were that he thought he could do better for Anthony than Celia was doing. She could not let it pass. Although she knew her father meant well, she was roused to defend herself. When did he expect to become a widower, in five years or ten? At that age, in his late eighties or nineties, was he going to be capable of day and night nursing and restraint of an incontinent and escapist strong mentally handicapped young man? Would he be able to provide a large secure open space for Anthony to run about in, and physiotherapy, and a number of extra staff, and essential locks on doors and unbendable bars on windows? Bernard back-tracked, Celia forgave him. It was nonetheless sad. They said goodbye sadly.

The idea that she had solved most of her problems at the Orchard was proving illusory. The Orchard was like a beneficial drug with damaging side effects. It was good for Anthony, but had driven wedges between herself and Alan,

179

herself and her father, and was forcing her to lie and lie again to her two healthy children.

Unfortunately for her, the healthiest children catch infections. Charlotte caught mumps and measles, and gave them to Paul, who also caught chickenpox. Celia had to book an appointment with Dr Ward, a new GP who had taken over from Dr Railton. The consequential questions worried her more than the well-being of Charlotte and Paul: had Dr Railton told Dr Ward about Anthony, would Anthony figure in her other children's notes, would Dr Ward be discreet, could she ask him if she was likely to pass on the infection to her son at the Orchard? In the end she did not mention Anthony, nor did Dr Ward, and she stayed at home until she was out of quarantine.

One more regrettable setback for Celia was Con Thornton's tiff with her 'old fool', meaning Ian, her husband, who took the view that Anthony Sturridge should not be 'buried alive' with a 'whole lot of loonies'. Con intended to reassure Celia by revealing her fierce disagreement with Ian, but her good intention had the effect it is famous for, and Celia wished she had not been told, had not been the bone of contention between the Thorntons, and that her son and his fate could not be spoken of in such brutal terms.

An exception to the rule of disasters breeding disasters was a letter she received from Sandy Wellingham. Celia had allowed Dot to spill the beans to her mother – she trusted both of them. And Sandy showed her appreciation of the situation by enclosing her letter et cetera in an envelope in which Dot was sending Celia a frivolous women's magazine.

The letter ran: 'You are a hundred per cent right to have handed over Anthony to the professionals. Your other children owe you a huge debt, whether or not they ever repay it. Take no notice of the sentimentalists and do-gooders, who will want to do you down. You deserve a second medal for valour. Hope money will help. No thanks, please. Love from your fan.' Clipped to the writing paper were two hundred pounds in five pound notes. Celia rang Dot from the Orchard to say how grateful she was, to send a message to her mother, and to say the mag was a bright spot in a cloudy sky.

Time passed, the hands of the clock raced round while she was looking the other way. Now years added inches to the stature of all three children – or perhaps the inches were borrowed from their father, who had started to shrink and stoop. Celia forgot her looks, had no use for make-up, and asked one of the nurses at St Hugh's to chop off her overgrown hair. She cooked obsessively in order to keep those at home as well as possible, and to take titbits to the Orchard for Anthony. She forced herself to eat for her strength's sake. She was learning to laugh at nothing, since she had not much to laugh at anywhere.

In the fifth and sixth years of Anthony's exile she was aware of a strange transposition. She could not stop it happening, and, stranger still, was not sure that she wanted to. Charlotte was getting on for ten, Paul was eight, and they were extremely close. They went to school together, likewise did their homework, played together, had understandings and giggly jokes, and were or seemed to Celia to be a somewhat exclusive pair. Of course they had latchkeys – their mother was out four days a week and their father for five. She sometimes did night duty at St Hugh's, she was the tiredest of housewives, no wonder the two children had discovered how to amuse themselves. Celia could reflect that she was succeeding in her aim to give them the childhood they deserved. She nonetheless had to fight against feeling shut out by their closeness. She also hoped she was wrong in sometimes thinking Charlotte and Paul were short of friends, and that, because she was always afraid of being found out, the atmosphere at The Homestead was never carefree.

To drop the children at school on weekdays and drive on was not a chore, although varying degrees of exhaustion lay ahead. She had horrors to attend to at St Hugh's, but also patients who came in unwell and left much better. She had friends there, anyway colleagues, she knew what she was doing and was good at it. Moreover, her deeper emotions were not stirred.

Her days at the Orchard were horrific, too. But she was a trained nurse and prepared for what she saw and often had to do. And to be with Anthony, now, when she was used to him, satisfied her, whether or not it had any satisfactory meaning for him. Their days were peculiarly empty. He resisted affectionate gestures, his hand held, his back patted, let alone an embrace or a kiss. She spent hours following him round the garden or sitting with another mother or two on a pouffe in a bare assembly room, watching him slapping his thighs or standing motionless, frowning and moaning. Toys were scarce – toys could be put to perilous uses. Music played gently, high class music which helped to counter the patients' unrhythmical symptoms. Sometimes Anthony greeted her by means of an individualistic signal, possibly by averting his head or by leading her on a chase, and on rare occasions she had a more or less intuitive sense that he was sorry to see her go. Those signals of his, if they were signals, were payment in full by her standards for all the hours she devoted to his cause.

Above all, at the Orchard she was out of range of outsiders' opinions of her way with Anthony. There were no lies or secrets to contend with. It was a sad place, but the so-called normal personnel somehow made it happy – and Celia gradually had to admit that she was happier amongst all the sadness than she was at home – she admitted it with qualifications.

That admission was feminine: it was connected with an adult of the opposite sex as well as a boy. Her romantic interest in Edward Speed crept up on her. Perhaps it was traceable to Con Thornton's girlish interrogation when she told her friends about the Orchard; but she did not recognise it for many more years. He had been her hero from the start; but romance was the last of the thousand things on her mind. It was only when she had grown almost accustomed to Anthony, to anxiety about the other members of her family, money and the shortage thereof, and her daily, weekly, yearly expenditure of effort – only then did she spare a thought for Edward's head of greying hair, the charming set of his teeth when he smiled, his well-fleshed warm hands, and his tireless vigour.

He became the agency of her covert sighs. She looked forward to seeing him, even if from a distance, to exchanging a word or two; but was aware of the remnants of shyness and was apt to blush when they did speak to each other. Sometimes, against her will, for fear of disappointment, she avoided him. Her emotion was a Dead Sea fruit; how could it be otherwise since she had unbreakable ties, and he was married to Mary Speed and they had children. Besides, in reality, she was no Eve, not tempted by 'the fruit that was forbidden', and was sure that he with his idealism, also his fulfilled countenance, felt the same. It was all a dream for her, escapism, something to balance her unsparing practicality.

They discussed Anthony, but not often, and there was not much to be said. Edward ran the Orchard and studied autism: those were his business and his priorities. If his patients were ill, they were attended by the resident nurses or by the local practice of GPs: no opportunity for Celia in such situations. Ill patients were kept at the Orchard: an autistic boy or youth in a general hospital presented unacceptable difficulties and expense. Anyway, Edward rose above ordinary health problems in order to have time for paperwork and fund raising, and to be able to stroll through his premises, distributing smiles like blessings.

So far, Anthony's constitution had not failed. He had grown out of his infantile beauty, his teeth had come in crooked but nobody wanted to try to put them in a plate, and his expression was tortured and not easy on the eye; but his physique was slim and tense, and he had not lost his power of attraction. Occasionally, in those long spells of watching over him, Celia half-wished that he might need medical attention of a sort that would bring her and Edward together. She visualised them in a semi-dark room at the San, leaning over Anthony in the bed, whispering caring sentiments in close proximity. Another wish, an inevitable wish that had dogged her from the day she discovered Anthony was not like other boys, she now censored absolutely, for a reason supportive of maternal considerations, because if Anthony were to die she would be separated for ever from Edward Speed.

She was interested in his wife. The Speeds lived in a house about a mile from the Orchard. Celia once drove past it: there was a high hedge in front, also a pig-wire fence, and closed metal gates – she could just see an upstairs bay window under a gable – the bedroom Edward shared with Mary – and a couple of smaller windows. She knew that Mary never came near her husband's place of work, and had heard on the grapevine

185

that she was scared of autistic boys: which must have accounted for the defences of her home. She imagined Mary would be quite pretty, and long-suffering on account of Edward's absenteeism from the family hearth, a limited person with little understanding of or sympathy with his work, probably a good cook because he looked well-fed, able to satisfy all his physical appetites, but not half good enough, judged by Celia's criteria.

She thought about her face as she had not done for ages. She even tried to look at herself in the bathroom. At a certain point she reverted to the application of a spot of lipstick. She was probably Edward's age, a few years older than Mary, but much more experienced. Her exertions had kept her figure trim, and miraculously her miseries had not transferred themselves to her complexion – her skin was tautened, not relaxed into creases and folds, and her eyes were lamplike.

She was not a flirt. She was not unfaithful to Alan. Her feelings for Edward resembled a secret garden, where she could roam without doing harm to anyone or anyone being harmed. For years they had behaved with perfect propriety, as two professionals engaged in making the life of a handicapped boy as tolerable as they could. Had he smiled at her with a mite more benevolence than he smiled at others, and had a spark of sexual electricity flashed between them? Those questions were not promises. They were simply a man and a woman, and propinquity told the rest of the story.

Anthony was now approaching puberty. At twelve years old his voice had begun to break. Celia knew that the step into manhood was fraught with dangers for autistic boys. In the winter he caught a cold. He had stayed out in the rain one evening, the Orchard people had been unable to persuade him to come in, and Celia was not there – it was a weekend. He was removed from his dormitory and kept in a room by himself in the San. He was clearly not happy, he was unaccustomed to and disliked the isolation. Celia kept him company when she could, but she too hated to be locked in, and disliked the aid-call or panic-button that she was required to hang round her neck.

Anthony got worse rather than better. His padding round his bedroom for the majority of every twenty-four hours, like an animal in the zoo, cannot have done him good. He developed a cough, a temperature, bronchitis, pneumonia – he now lay in bed, wheezing instead of moaning, staring at the ceiling, alternatively sweating and shivering. He had never been anywhere near so ill. Considering his autistic capabilities, he was quiet and co-operative.

Celia obtained permission from Alan and St Hugh's to spend extra time at the Orchard. She sat by Anthony's bed, speaking to him, wiping his hot forehead with a cool damp towel, spreading another blanket over him, trying to persuade him to drink water or soup, attending to his needs. The crisis lasted for the inside of a week. She stayed late for five evenings, when the nurses were busy getting the other boys to bed. Edward Speed joined her for ten minutes or so on each of them.

He arrived at about nine o'clock. They talked a little through the masks they both had to wear, and communicated more by their eyes. She thanked him, and he said he was always worried by pneumonia – Celia knew what he meant. She expressed concern for his wife and children, and he shook his head. He took Anthony's pulse, and when Celia asked if her son was going to die he shrugged his shoulders. She wished they could talk properly, at length, and not in the room in which Anthony might be giving up the ghost – she knew Edward through and through, but only metaphorically. He patted her on the shoulder, she touched and squeezed his warm hand. One night he said that Anthony would have been a splendid person but for the autism, and she loved Edward for that.

The disease burned itself out, perhaps literally with a sky-high temperature. Celia waited until Edward came in on the sixth evening, so that she could show him Anthony asleep, breathing more easily, not flushed, not restive. Edward led her out of the room by the hand and along the passages to his consulting room. Most of the ground floor of the building was empty at this hour. They had taken off their masks but were not yet speaking to each other. He shut the door of his room behind them, and opened his arms for Celia to almost fall into, saying how glad he was, how relieved she must be, what a splendid vigil she had maintained, and that she had to take some credit for the outcome.

Their embrace began as a hug, but extended into closer contact. Then she kissed his cheek, murmuring grateful words, and he kissed hers. And then it was lips, and a proper kiss, a kiss with passion thrown in by both parties, and hungry movements of heads and daring caresses of hands.

Celia broke away.

She said: 'No – I can't – sorry – it was lovely!'

He said: 'Nor can I – but thank you.'

They laughed into each other's faces.

She said she would have to go home, and he said so would he.

He said: 'I think the world of you – honestly – my kiss was a tribute.'

'I could say the same,' she replied.

'You're an amazing person, I've never known anyone like you, so pretty, and strong at the same time. I haven't seen you cry while Anthony's been ill, or before that, not once – most mothers of the boys shed tears constantly.'

'I haven't shed mine yet,' she replied, laughing. 'I've had better things to do. Look – this evening was exceptional – we mustn't muddle ourselves up.'

'I agree. It's a bargain. I'm sorry if I've muddled you.'

'You haven't. You've given me a great boost. I know there are clouds on my horizon, and I'll be needing your encouragement. But I promise not to be a nuisance.'

'You wouldn't ever be that. You're the odd woman out. Good night, sleep well.'

They kissed chastely, and he accompanied her to the exit.

The clouds Celia knew about referred to pneumonia for pubescent autistic males and its fatal implications.

She had learned the facts of life for boys like Anthony from books and the professional staff at the Orchard, and mainly from the women in her situation. Now she recognised their last common denominator, the probable early loss of their afflicted ones.

The sky was not altogether blacked out by the clouds. For Anthony, death could surely be described by the platitude, a merciful release. What had adult life to offer him? No freedom, no sex, no work, no hope – in short, no fun. It was hard to believe that he would be better off alive than dead, that was the truth; and she was too sensible not to acknowledge it.

As for the rest, his death would be a panacea. The money problem would be solved. Celia would not be exhausted. Alan would no longer be impaled on the horns of his dilemma. Charlotte and Paul would not be bombs timed to explode as soon as they began to meddle with the mystery of Anthony, the Sturridges could mingle with the Farrs at Broadstairs, the children's grandparents could ask questions till the cows came home, and sociability and hospitality would again be on the cards. Celia could probably afford to stop work altogether and become a proper mother and a good wife to her husband in his retirement. Hard-boiled analysis could claim in its post mortem that Anthony had been a cuckoo in the nest.

Yet the words on the relevant maternal lips that quivered were negative – no, not quite so soon, mercy, pax! The heart is not an analyst. Celia rebelled against her son's sentence that might be carried out on any day. Anthony did not deserve to die. Did she deserve to lose him? She appealed against the verdict of nature. She pleaded for an extension of his life. She would miss him unbearably. She was desperate to be with him as much as possible or more than was possible.

He had pulled through pneumonia. She had helped him, she was proud of him, and, on the way home after Edward Speed and she had kissed and come to terms, she was in a celebratory mood. Marvellous things had happened. But a few miles from the Orchard she had to pull into a lay-by on the road because she was blinded by tears. It was a storm of sorrow, and subsided quickly. She remembered that she had to smile and laugh for Anthony's sake, and Alan's, Charlotte's, Paul's, and the world's.

She felt incapable, but overcame the feeling. She was able to tell Alan that Anthony was well again – and Alan was glad. She slept then. That night and the next, and if she ever sat down in the daytime, she recouped the sleep she had

missed. She drank coffee before she drove anywhere, and more coffee to keep herself awake at
St Hugh's and back at the Orchard. Her sleep
was not just the opposite of wakefulness; she
knew in her bones it was also a kind of preparation.
Her constitution was gathering its forces.

She and Alan agreed to play down her
absenteeism from The Homestead so as not to
worry Charlotte and Paul and arouse curiosity.
There had been an epidemic, a lot of illness,
and their mother had provided extra nursing,
they said. They specified nothing, who was ill
and where, and the children swallowed the story
without demur. Charlotte was more than ever
preoccupied by crushes on girls and teachers at
school, and Paul was mad on cricket and moved
from Point A to Point B only aided by the
motions of a fast bowler.

Another agreement with Alan smoothed her
path. He indicated that he was aware of Anthony's
critical illness, and raised no objections to her
stealing off to the Orchard even during weekends.

She was able to see Anthony in the San as
she could not have seen him if he had been in
a dormitory. She would arrive with the dawn,
and leave him in the night. She could let herself
into his room. She could talk to him – he was
at last her captive audience – or watch over him
as he lay in bed, drowsing or asleep.

She told him everything. Although he never
answered, he was her confessor and her judge.
She held nothing back. Quietly, in order not to
be overheard, even in a whisper, she entertained

192

him like Scheherazade: the difference was that Scheherazade told her tales to postpone her execution, whereas Celia told hers to postpone his. She reminisced about Thanet Steps, her childhood, her parents, Dot and Con. She described Owen Pennant, and the frenzy of their love-making at Biarritz, and becoming hardly more than his hostess and housekeeper at home, and then the horror of his adultery with that squalid woman, engaged in an act so extremely intimate, and painful for a wife to witness.

She spoke of her clean cuts, first by leaving Owen, then by leaving Anthony himself at the Orchard. She had acted spontaneously, abruptly, but was still convinced she was right. Owen proved he was a traitor, and one betrayal was enough to convince her that she could never again depend on him: what sort of a marriage would theirs have been, what would it have been worth? People criticised her inflexibility: to keep your word, and expect the man to whom you had given yourself body and soul to keep his, was better than compromise, a marriage based on immorality or feebleness or money – she would rather be inflexible than degraded.

She was sorry, she said, that she had torn Anthony away from his sister and brother and that he had not seen his father since he was tiny. But she had acted unselfishly, for his sake, because the world would not understand him or treat him with respect, and to protect three other people, his father, Charlotte and Paul. Although she was a nurse, she could not have nursed him

193

all day and all night: she had to be a wife, a mother of the other two, and keep house. She lacked the strength, it would have been impossible, whatever ignorance and the happy-go-lucky bleeding-heart brigade might think and say.

She asked for absolution. She asked to be forgiven.

He was more amenable when he was not well. Sometimes he let her hold his hand or lay her cool hand on his hot forehead. She could not kiss him with her mask on, but she pressed their foreheads together. His puberty had been delayed by the pneumonia, his voice remained half-broken, and he had not reached manhood in other ways. He was a boy still. Admittedly the beauty of his childhood had been replaced by features that betrayed his illness, frown-lines between his eyebrows, a sharp nose, tightly compressed lips, and always the anxious expression; but his eyes were bigger and bluer than they used to be, and they seemed to Celia to have acquired a beautiful new expressiveness. She thought he spoke through his eyes. She wondered if they had begun to communicate through their eyes.

The days passed, the months, a year, then another half-year – borrowed time. Celia did not tire of being with Anthony, tiring as it was in the ordinary sense. The kaleidoscope had been moved. Her love had altered. It was connected no more with guilt or uncertainty. It was unworldly, it was other-worldly, if such a word or state existed, she would say to herself. And the object of it was not the same as he had been, when she suspected him of malice. There was no more violence in him.

His health improved, and Celia was happy in a way when he was considered fit to rejoin the other boys. Her preference always was for him to be as normal and free as possible. Soon he would be back in the San, which, again in a way, was sad. Yet she loved to have him to herself, and his eyes seemed to register passivity and even perhaps acceptance of his lot. He surely listened to her autobiographical confidences, and she thought he at least appreciated the sound of her voice. She felt so close to him in their sessions in the San that she could not help imagining or hoping that he had comparable feelings. Could it be that he had served his time in the purgatory of disease? Could he be emerging from his chrysalis? She tried not to be both hopeful and fearful simultaneously – it was too contradictory – yet the emotions were combined since, if he rose from his form of being dead, he would not have time to realise his full potential.

Her love confused her. She was mothering her child, although he was nearly grown up. She was preoccupied by an affair of the heart, although it was unilateral as well as platonic. She was taking from Alan, Charlotte and Paul to give to one who had almost nothing to give her. Nevertheless, now and increasingly, her confusion was superseded by admiration of Anthony. He might only be a fragment of a person, but he had qualities – an individuality, an integrity –

which she fancied had been acquired by some heroic psychological effort. He seemed wise to her, and in his presence, against all odds, she experienced peace.

She tried to explain it all to Edward Speed, who had been supporting her through the ups and downs of Anthony's vicissitudes.

He commented: 'I've heard similar stories before ... I wonder who is developing, the autistic child or the parent? ... Scepticism is all very well, but has its limits ... Anything can happen, and usually does ... Don't lose your nerve!'

Another assistant at the Orchard, Alyson, who was friendly with Celia, reinforced Edward's views. She inquired one day, while they watched the boys, Anthony included, mooning about in the garden: 'Do you ever think they're clever, cleverer than they look, cleverer than we are?'

Anthony's health had taken another turn for the better, which had side effects at The Homestead. Celia spent more time there. Alan was relieved. Charlotte and Paul received an extra share of attention.

She would praise Alan when they were alone in their bedroom at night. She said she had been too busy and tired to run through the whole list of her reasons to love him. She did so, bit by bit, while he tried not to go to sleep. He had caused her no tremors over unknown girls at the office. He had not beaten her. He had made bread for the family without fail. He had followed her into the maze of care of Anthony, and reassured her hundreds of times that they were not lost. He had been a gentleman and a brick. His only serious fault was that he kept on growing older.

Celia's fault-finding was lightly said, yet was no joke. Alan was old beyond his years, slower in all respects, more pedantic and harder of hearing. He added to her catalogue of dreads. Without him, to put it bluntly, her life would fall apart. She would have less time for Anthony. She would have no buffer between herself and Charlotte and Paul, who might begin to ask the unanswerable questions. And she would be doing all the practical things he had done.

As she ceased to concentrate on nothing but Anthony, who was apparently on a road to relative recovery, she was reminded that life was short not only for Alan. Her father rang to say that her mother was in hospital. Chrissy had been taken ill without warning, and had been diagnosed with rampant cancer. She was seventy-eight. She was aware of her condition. She was philosophical, not suffering intolerable symptoms, and was coming home on the next day. She would like to see her daughter and her grandchildren. Bernard was sorry not to have contacted Celia before, but everything had happened in a rush. He himself was okay, and could manage Chrissy with help from a District Nurse.

Celia rearranged everything, prepared a picnic lunch, and drove Charlotte and Paul to Thanet Steps. They spent half an hour with Chrissy between twelve-thirty and one o'clock. Chrissy was in the double bed in the Farrs' bedroom, and the curtains were partly drawn to shut out light. She looked bad, but behaved well, uttered no complaints, smiled with grace and courage, even laughed with the children. Bernard shared Celia's picnic lunch in the dining-room, and kept the children with him when Celia went upstairs afterwards.

Her mother spoke gratefully of the past. She praised her husband and even said that her daughter had become a fine woman. Her one reference to Anthony was not critical of his treatment.

She said: 'Poor boy! You've done the best you could for him, and borne your cross.'

Celia thanked her for saying so.

'We've had our differences,' Chrissy continued. 'Forgive me!'

'Of course, Mother. Forgive me, please!'

'Yes, yes. Perhaps I'll meet Anthony in heaven.'

'Perhaps, yes.'

'If I get there.'

They both laughed, and Celia kissed her goodbye in the dim room.

She had a short talk with her father. He was sleeping in the spare room. He expected Chrissy to be admitted to a local hospice in a few days time. Her wishes were being observed. He said he was coping and that he would be all right. She promised to come to Broadstairs if she possibly could whenever needed.

Six days later she received the news that Chrissy had died at home. Bernard said she had gone to sleep and not woken – it had been more like a petal dropping than a death. They discussed the funeral. She would return to stay at Broadstairs for the night before her mother was cremated, and stay for that night too; also prepare tea for the mourners. She would notify Dot Tyler and Con Thornton. She would do all her travelling by train, so that Alan could drive the children down for the service and get them back to Highgate.

After it was nearly all over, and Alan and most of the guests had departed, Celia had a word with her father, then led Dot and Con upstairs, to her own room in the attic where they had conferred in the old days. The same posters were pinned on the walls, and some of her baby books remained in the bookshelf. Dot lay on the bed, Con sat on the ottoman in front of the window, and Celia on her little chair by the child's desk.

They spoke of death. They spoke of parents and husbands. Dot asked after Anthony Sturridge tentatively. Celia told the truth, and was sympathised with.

Then Dot said: 'Would it be better for all concerned...?'

'Probably.'

'What does that mean?'

'I've grown so fond of him. I'd miss him so much.'

'Is it horrid for you to talk of what happens after Anthony?'

'No – I don't mind – with you. I have nightmares about what happens then.'

'You'll be freed.'

199

'Will I? Alan's not very strong. You saw today how much older he looks.'

'But you'll have more time to be with Charlotte and Paul.'

'Yes. I hardly know them. We'll have to try to make friends from scratch.'

Con asked: 'Have you had any happiness with Alan?'

'Oh yes – not ecstatic – ecstatic's a caution, I was ecstatic with Owen – but Alan is slippers by the fire, and sweet and kind – everything in our garden was lovely until I realised Anthony was ill.'

'No happiness after that?'

'Rays of sunshine through storm clouds.'

'Can I ask you a really personal question?'

'You always do, we always do – and we're still friends.'

'Have you looked to right or left?'

'I was kissed and kissed back once – it was magical.'

Dot said: 'Only once? That's tragic – terrific kisses are the beginning of a story in real life – they're only the end in novels.'

'Neither of us could do adultery.'

Con said: 'You're awfully moral, Celia.'

'Is that a confession? Have you strayed?'

'A bit. No, more than a bit.'

'Happily?'

'It's been good for me and for dear old Ian. Actually, Ian's responsible without meaning to be. He bought a second sofa, and I fell for the delivery man. He's young. He's exciting. We meet in the back of his van – there's always a sofa there. He makes up for the change of life.'

'What's he called?' Dot asked.

'Vince.'

'You're not going to bolt, are you?'

'Good gracious, no! Ian is quite old, literally, and he'd be high and dry without me. I wouldn't have looked twice at Vince if it hadn't been for the change – I wanted to have some fun before it was curtains – I married too young – and there was no one else for donkey's years. Have you started changing?'

'I started and stopped, or seemed to – I haven't noticed symptoms lately,' Celia replied.

'What about you, Dot?' Con asked.

'I'm getting flushes. My naughty husband's gone to write a book in Alaska, he said he was distracted by having to open and close windows for me. Adultery might freshen up my marriage – isn't that what's said about it? But I can't be bothered. I've got my Adam, and I'm lucky to be rich – money can answer a lot of prayers, as Celia's discovered.'

'Largely thanks to you and your mother, Dot.'

Con said: 'I wish I'd helped you more,' and Celia replied: 'You would have if you could.'

They began to worry that they should go downstairs to be with Bernard Farr.

They talked about health briefly, Dot's migraines, Con's weight problem, and Celia's exertions.

Dot remarked: 'I've found out what would have happened to your Anthony if you'd kept him at home. You would have had to drug him, use tranquillisers and stronger stuff. My Adam's taught me how exhausting straightforward children are. You'd have been a dead duck if Anthony was let loose on you, and so would your other children, I guess. I hope Charlotte and Paul never forget that.'

Con asked: 'Was your kisser that doctor at the Orchard?'

Celia replied: 'You've got a memory like an elephant,' and Con commented ruefully: 'Not just my memory's like an elephant.'

Anthony Sturridge died five days after his Farr grandmother's funeral.

Late in the evening of the day of Chrissy's funeral, when Celia and her father were preparing to go upstairs and to bed, Alan rang through with the news that Anthony was in the San at the Orchard with a chest infection. Dr Speed had telephoned the information. Alan realised that Celia would want to know without delay, but was sorry to have to tell her in such already sad circumstances.

She was paralysed by the shock for a few minutes. She knew he would die – Edward would not have rung if the infection had not been terminal. That she had expected it seemed not to ameliorate the shock.

She had answered the telephone in the hall of 42 Thanet Steps. She rejoined her father in the sitting-room. He looked at her face, stood up, supported her to a chair.

'Is it Anthony?' he asked.

She nodded.

'Is he dead?'

'Soon will be,' she replied.

He made her a cup of tea with lots of sugar. He brought it to her and begged her to drink.

'How can I get to the Orchard?' she asked.

It was a tricky question. There might be a midnight train from Broadstairs to London; but she would arrive upsettingly late at The Homestead, and the same applied to her arrival in the small hours at the Orchard – and how would Alan and the children cope without the family car? She did not want to ring Alan again – he would probably say he would drive to Broadstairs at once and transport her to the Orchard – leaving Charlotte and Paul alone. Her father offered to drive her there, but he was eighty-seven, or lend her his car, but how was he to recover it?

She agreed to wait for a morning train. The argument that convinced was that Anthony might be worried if she turned up at his bedside in the middle of the night.

She did her best to hide her frantic feelings from her father, told him she would try to snatch some sleep, reminded him that he was worn out and had better do the same. She would leave the house early without disturbing him.

He revealed that her face after she had spoken on the telephone had given him the jim-jams. He was okay now. They must both rest, at least. He would be longing for a bulletin about Anthony.

She left the house at five a.m. on the next day. She arrived at the Orchard at eleven, having been delayed by having to mend a tear in Paul's school blazer and to ring and explain why she was unable to work at St Hugh's. She spent hours in Anthony's familiar room in the San on that day and the four others.

He was paler, thinner, sleepier. He breathed with difficulty, yet could sleep through his feeble coughing. Sometimes an attempt was made to give him oxygen, but he hated the mask and nobody wanted to hold it forcibly over his nose and mouth. Apparently he was not in pain. Edward told Celia that he and Dr Timms, the GP in charge, had agreed that morphia as required, but no antibiotics, should be administered. She could not object.

She talked to Anthony, as before. She felt that they were communicating somehow. She was sorry to have been absent while her mother was buried. She said that his grandfather had stood up to the obsequies stoically. She discussed her parents' marriage with him, and Bernard's love of Chrissy, who drove most people demented. She told him that his father, Alan, had worked tremendously hard to pay for the Orchard – he had been too busy on Anthony's account to come and see him. She declared her love repeatedly, and now she removed her mask to kiss his forehead. He did not respond, or did he? She could not be sure if the flicker of his eyelids, or the slight opening of his eyes, or a jerk of his hand, meant anything much. It no longer mattered, she reflected.

In the evening of the fifth day she was convinced that her good night was also goodbye. She had to leave him – she had promised Alan and the others that she would be coming home.

Edward rang her there. The details of Anthony's passing were not too harrowing. Celia cried in Alan's arms, and his feelings of failure, because he had not braved the Orchard, came to a painful crux. They told each other that they had done their best for their ill boy, but neither of them seemed to believe that their best was adequate. Grief notwithstanding, Celia suspected that Alan was as nervous as she was of having to provide explanations for Charlotte and Paul.

Charlotte was at the awkward age in girls, between sixteen and seventeen. She was clever at school, but had not won the lottery for looks. She had inherited Alan's long face and high-bridged nose, and Celia's straight blonde hair that looked like rats' tails when Charlotte allowed it to reach her shoulders. She had an odd figure, big breasts and a fat waist. And she was greedy and overweight. Her lack of physical attraction was not balanced by the charm of an angelic character.

Paul at fourteen was giggly and cuddly, and better looking than his sister – his face was a masculine reworking of his mother's, and he had some of her agility; he was also bad at his books and had an unexpected obstinate streak.

Charlotte was close to Alan, they had always been close, and she was now critical of, rude to, and grumpy with Celia. Paul on the other hand was not very nice to Alan, he treated him like a relic of the past, while his manner towards his mother was indulgent and patronising.

Alan took it on himself to tell the children at breakfast.

'We've had sad news,' he said. 'Your brother has been very ill, and last night he lost his battle.'

Charlotte asked in a brutal way: 'Is Anthony dead?'

Paul asked with his mouth full of cereal: 'What's happened?'

Celia explained: 'Poor Anthony died.'

'Our Anthony?'

'Yes, Paul.'

'Well – I don't remember him.'

Charlotte chipped in sharply: 'Well, I do.'

Alan said: 'I'm afraid we'll have another funeral in a few days. Your mother and I feel there's no need for you to be there. Neither of you were able to know Anthony, unfortunately. I myself did not see him in the last few years. We'd understand if you chose to stay away. You've both got work to do at school.'

'Why did he die?' Charlotte demanded.

Alan hesitated, then said: 'He had an incurable condition.'

Celia interrupted: 'I'd prefer not to be dragged into Anthony's medical history. Please let's leave all that for another day. You two can think about the funeral. I must be off, I've many other duties to attend to.'

Paul said: 'I'm not going to any more funerals.'

Charlotte weighed in resentfully: 'Where's

Anthony now? Where's he been? You might tell us that.'

'Please, Charlotte,' Alan said, 'please spare your mother – she's in mourning twice over.'

At this point Celia left the breakfast table. Later, without seeing the children again because they were at school, nor Alan because she had encouraged him to keep an appointment in Highgate, she drove to the Orchard.

Edward met her, and nurses and a few other mothers crowded round to console. She spent a little time with Anthony in a cold room that was new to her: but it was too sad to see him looking so well for a change and dead. The secretary in the office, Kirsty, talked to an undertaker who was willing and able to arrange a cremation. Celia chose two hymns, *All things bright and beautiful*, and *God be in my head*.

She was not sure what to do next: everybody was so busy. She sat in a lobby for visitors, and that kind acquaintance of hers, Alyson, passed by and stopped to commiserate with her.

Celia said: 'I mustn't keep you, you'll need to look after your boy.'

'Oh no, my dear,' Alyson replied, 'I lost my boy four years ago.'

Celia was sorry and sympathetic, she explained that she had assumed Alyson worked at the Orchard for the same reason she had done so.

'I couldn't stop coming here,' Alyson explained in her turn; 'I wanted to be where John had been, and help the other boys. The Orchard's been my saving grace as well as John's. I wonder if it would be good for you.'

They said goodbye.

For Celia, a ray of light tentatively broke through the darkness of recent days. She could reconnect with Anthony by working for autistic children. She could shelter under the wing of Edward Speed. She would be useful, occupied, and to some extent protected from her children. The stunning effect of Anthony's death wore off slightly. She had been exhausted before he died, she had years and years of exhaustion accumulating inside her, and when he was gone the remnants of her strength seemed to go with him. Now she sensed the possibility of recovery.

But driving back to Highgate in the car, in the autumn, she realised that if she were to work at the Orchard without the excuse of Anthony, she would have to tell her children the truth about his autism. She would have to confess to having told them lies. She might have to organise a tour of inspection of the Orchard, where autism would give a grim account of itself to ignorant youth. She foresaw misunderstanding, criticism, quarrels, and that Charlotte and Paul were going to be as difficult as their brother or more so.

The falling leaves were like a metaphor. Other metaphors occurred to her: pigeons were coming home to roost, she had sown a wind and had to reap a whirlwind. The idea that supported her was that Anthony had had worse luck.

His funeral was awful. Charlotte's mood took precedence over Celia's grief. Bernard Farr had offered to attend, but Celia had begged him not to. She had been afraid that he would scold Paul for obstinately hiding at school, and then she was thankful that he did not witness Charlotte's sulky demeanour. She wanted to keep Bernard and Charlotte apart for as long as she could – she was sure he would answer the questions Charlotte was likely to ask.

That evening she sought Alan's assistance in her new trouble. They were in their bedroom, he was already in bed. He said they should inform the children fully and without reserve, and that he would share with her any blame or aspersions that were cast on the struggle to provide them with a normal upbringing.

She replied: 'You won't be blamed, blame's reserved for mothers.'

He smiled at her nonsense. Charlotte and Paul would come round to appreciating all she had done for her three children.

'When?' she asked. 'I'll lose meanwhile or for ever. They're angry with me already for telling them half the story, and they'll be angrier if or when I tell the other half.'

'You exaggerate, my dear,' he said.

'And you don't know, Alan. What about heredity – they'll have that hanging over them – will they have autistic children? There's a money problem, there's public opinion –'

'My dear,' he interrupted her, 'it's late, you're tired, we've had a long wretched day – shouldn't we be thinking of Anthony rather than ourselves and what our other children might think of us?'

She did not answer back. She was silenced and crushed not only by the funeral, the attitude of Charlotte and Paul, the discordant atmosphere in her home, and Alan's unjust rebuke, but also the preceding years.

She kissed her husband good night. He had done his best for Anthony, but she was not in the mood to be lectured, and had to admit to herself that she was fed up with his limitations. His 'thoughts' for his dead son did not compensate for shunning that son when he was alive.

Alan slept while she lay awake, picturing her life as she had lived it, with marriages and mother-hood included. Honesty brushed out illusions. Her husbands had not understood or loved her really, and two of her children were against her. As for the third, had she meant anything to his autism?

Day dawned, days were got through. Charlotte was occupied with her schooling and did not revert to the subject of Anthony, and Paul played football and cricket and seemed to have consigned him to oblivion. Celia explained to Edward Speed why she could not come to the Orchard for the time being, and had offered extra services to St Hugh's. She could not face being more at home: setting aside the deteriorating atmosphere, Alan was scheduled to retire in a matter of weeks and she was not looking forward to keeping him company round the clock.

One day she availed herself of Dot's standing invitation to join her for a bite of lunch. They ate sausages and mash with twelve-year-old Adam

Tyler, a hungry type who left them to join in a friendly rugger match.

Dot inquired, 'Are you all right?'

Celia replied: 'No – yes – I'm so all wrong that I can't begin to tell you.'

'You have begun – go on!'

'I'm being eaten alive by doubts that I did well for Anthony.'

'What parts have they eaten so far?'

'Should I have had that operation on my Fallopian tubes earlier? Did I endanger my children by postponing it?'

'If you hadn't postponed, wouldn't you have had little Pennants, who'd now be racing about in Mercs and endangering the rest of us?'

'I suppose so. And I wouldn't have liked that.'

'Anthony was a mystery, luck's a mystery, and so's life – and the poor boy's story is water under the bridge, isn't it? Forgive me for being bracing. We relied on you because you weren't doubtful. You took a brave decision, and we've been proud of you.'

'Perhaps I wasn't right to spirit Anthony away.'

'Who's been telling you that?'

'My surviving children know more than they did – we had to let them come to the funeral – they have a little knowledge and it's being dangerous.'

'How?'

'Charlotte's angry with me, and Paul's not very nice. We haven't had a row or anything yet. Charlotte's at college, she hasn't time to pick a quarrel, and Paul only thinks of ball games –

211

he's that age. The atmosphere at home is so bad, Dot! The air should be clearer, but I haven't the nerve to tackle the children.'

'You think they'll think autism's a stigma or a curse?'

'They're sure to think I was cruel to Anthony. But I wasn't – I loved him more than I loved them – and I was trying to be kind to everyone. Sorry to sound – and be – so feeble. Anthony's death has had a bad effect all round – Charlotte and Paul used to be biddable and on my side, and now they're my enemies.'

'Autism isn't a shameful thing – it's just frightfully difficult to live with – you can get doctors to confirm it. What does Alan advise?'

'Oh dear – Alan's at a disadvantage when it comes to Anthony – he only visited Anthony once at Orchard Grange.'

'Good grief! Once in all those years?'

'He couldn't bear it. He couldn't bear references to Anthony. Now he shuts up when I try to talk about Anthony. He won't be helpful when the crunch comes. It's not altogether his fault.'

'Why do you say that?

'He doesn't know all. Nobody knows all.'

'What is all? I don't want to probe – but you know I can keep a secret.'

'The secret is that I haven't any defence against my children. Orchard Grange was my decision. It was based on my beliefs. My beliefs are arguable. Even the belief that swung my decision could be contested. I seemed to have reason to believe that Anthony had a killer instinct.'

'What?'

'You heard, Dot. I think he endangered the life of Paul. And I think he killed our canary – it was called Timmy. And he nearly killed us both in the car.'

'Oh Celia, poor you!'

'Apparently he showed no sign of that symptom later on. He was always supervised at the Orchard. I might have been mistaken.'

'You couldn't have kept him at home anyway. He'd have ruined all your lives.'

'That's a matter of opinion. You know what liberals are. I've told you my biggest problem, but it's bred little ones.'

'Such as?'

'Alan, for one – he's on the point of retirement – he'll be at home all day for seven days a week – and I can't rely on him to resist Charlotte's curiosity and stand up for me. He wasn't a broken reed when we married. He was broken little by little by Anthony. He'd have been dead long ago if I'd insisted on keeping Anthony at home – but that's only my opinion, again.'

'Are you postponing the evil hour of pouring out your heart to Charlotte and Paul?'

'Yes – roughly speaking – I'm postponing the possibility of another family disaster – just until the children are a bit older and wiser. Do you think that's another mistake?'

'Your situation's so tricky, everything you do or don't do could be a mistake. I'm not offering you advice – I just back you to solve your riddle, or rather riddles. I'm sorry for everything, Alan not least.'

'Oh – he's fine in himself – my other worry, in the same category, is my father. He's alone, a widower and aged, and I should ask him to stay in Highgate or take my family to Broadstairs, but I know there'd be talk of Anthony and I'd be in the dock … I'll be miserable if he's ill or dies. Dot, I've bent your ear for too long.'

'That's friendship for old girls. Carry on if you want.'

'No – I've done – and thanks for listening to me. Are you as well as you look?'

'Fingers crossed! I married a footloose scribe instead of a wandering knight, but oddly enough Jason fits the bill, he lets me get on with my life, and Adam and I have so few interests in common that we can't disagree.'

'I'm afraid I haven't read Jason's books.'

'Don't worry. He hopes his books never fall into the hands of family and friends because they never read them – or buy them for that matter.'

'You do read them though, don't you Dot?'

'Of course – on pain of death – with torture thrown in if I criticise a single word. Luckily, Jason's books are good, and he can sometimes write them within reach of me.'

They laughed and kissed goodbye and Dot promised to pass everything on to Con.

Again time passed at The Homestead. The volcano continued to smoke, but did not erupt. Celia often wore black clothes to remind her children that she had been bereaved and was not

214

fit to be taken to task. There were two celebrations, which, she hoped, were not turned into damp squibs by her half-heartedness. The first was Charlotte's eighteenth birthday. Her parents gave her a present of money and a dinner party for thirty, a mix of old school friends and the new friends she had made at college, who were dingy and eventually drunken.

The second celebration was to mark Alan's retirement. Carter Johnssen made a presentation of a silver rose bowl at a drinks party after work, to which Celia and the children were invited, and then Alan asked a dozen of his colleagues and business pals in for a buffet supper at home. Celia did her best to be sociable, and might have done better if Mr Carter had not told her to keep a sharp eye on Alan because he had been looking poorly.

In the ensuing days she noticed that Alan slept a lot. He dropped off over the newspaper and as soon as he had switched on the TV. He was looking his age, or even more than his age; but he had had a difficult life what with May and then an autistic son. She urged him to go for long walks and keep fit.

She had her father rather than her husband on her mind. Bernard had fallen over in Thanet Steps, the street, not in 42. He had broken no bones, only grazed an elbow and bruised a knee, but was feeling under par. She asked St Hugh's if she could take leave of absence for three days, bought supplies of food for Alan and the children, and escaped to Broadstairs.

She and her father were happy to be together again. They both said they had longed for a meeting. That led into why they had not met since the day after Chrissy's funeral. Celia's apology became an explanation, and gradually she also entrusted Bernard with her secrets. He urged her to grasp the nettle of telling the children the truth or a tactfully edited version of it.

She thanked him. She was inclined to agree with him. But when she left him and was in the train to London, she disagreed. Her father had failed to appreciate the intricacies of her situation and the characters of Charlotte and Paul. She could not teach them the history of seventeen extraordinary years in an hour or so, she would not try, instead she would answer the questions she was bound to be asked sooner or later. She would give the children the information they were seeking, but nothing superfluous to their requirements. She would wait to be asked. She was choosing now to hold her peace, whereas previously she was driven by fear to keep quiet. She trusted her father to understand and not to interfere.

She arrived at The Homestead at lunchtime. She was due at St Hugh's at two o'clock and to work there until ten at night. She found Alan asleep in his chair in the sitting-room, and no food prepared in the kitchen. She woke him and said she would cook scrambled eggs and bacon in the kitchen. She was depressed by her reception.

He came into the kitchen and said he was sorry. He slumped down in a kitchen chair and supported his head in his hand by resting his elbow on the table. She told him not to worry, she was glad he had got his forty winks.

'No,' he said. 'No, my dear Celia, it's not that, although I am sorry not to have provided lunch.'

'What is it then? Are you ill?'

'I've told the children everything.'

'You haven't!'

'They wormed it out of me. I believe it's a good thing, but I'm sorry because I know I've gone against your wishes. I'm convinced that in time they will see that you acted in everyone's best interests.'

'Oh dear! Did I act without your consent? Don't answer – it doesn't matter. I take it the children were upset?'

'Temporarily, yes.'

'How upset?'

'They've decided to stay with Charlotte's friends for a few days, the Timbles – Jane Timble came to Charlotte's birthday party. They wanted time to adjust to Anthony's illness and his fate.'

'You mean they didn't want to see me.'

'No, my dear, not particularly that, they wanted time together in which to adjust.'

'They walked out on me.'

'No, my dear.'

'How could you, Alan? I warned you. I knew what would happen. You've stolen my children from me.'

'Oh, no, no no...'

'Yes yes!'

She left the kitchen. She cried upstairs until

a quarter to two. He had knocked on the bedroom door but she had said she had to be by herself. She went to the hospital. While she performed her duties mechanically, she posed and reposed the question, 'What next, what next?'

An answer of a sort was the news that her husband was in the hospital, in A and E, after collapsing in Paradise Street with a massive heart attack.

Alan Sturridge did not survive. He had been unconscious when he was stretchered into St Hugh's, and he did not regain consciousness.

Celia dealt with unavoidable paperwork at the hospital and was escorted home by Ellen, another nurse, a colleague. They drank cups of tea in The Homestead, and Celia had to account for the absence of the children – the two children, Ellen had no knowledge of the third.

'They're staying the night with people who live locally,' she said.

'Do you want to tell them about their father?'

'It's too late, it's nearly midnight.'

'Can I do anything? Would you like me to ring the people the children are staying with?'

'No, thanks. There'd be no point. I'm in no hurry to break the news.'

'You're so calm, Celia – I don't know how you can be so calm.'

'Forgive me for saying, that's what you think. But I could be getting used to death. Alan's the third person who was close to me who's died recently.'

'I'm very sorry.'

'So am I.'

'Would you like me to spend the night with you?'

'It's kind of you, but no, I'd rather be alone.'

'Well, I'd better be going back to work.'

'Shall I drive you to the hospital?'

'Don't bother, I like walking. How long were you married to Alan?'

'Nineteen years.'

'You'll miss him. I've been married to Jack for twice as long, and I hate to think how lonely I'll be without him. He's got a heart, as the cardiac people say.'

'Alan didn't seem to be ill. I was expecting my father to die, not my husband.'

'We all have regrets, don't we?'

'True! Thank you, Ellen.'

Celia wondered: what regrets could Ellen have? Surely none so sharp as hers!

Throughout the night she was tormented by waking nightmares. One was the memory of the reproaches she had heaped on Alan's head mere hours before his death, the hardest words she had ever addressed to him, that probably caused his heart attack. The other was Charlotte and Paul's rejection of and flight from their mother.

She rang the Timbles' telephone number at seven o'clock – it was not too early by normal standards. Nobody answered for many minutes. She was about to ring off when a sleepy froggy female voice came on the line.

'Is that Mrs Timble?' Celia asked.

'What's the time?'

'It's seven o'clock, Mrs Timble. I'm Celia Sturridge.'

'Oh God! Sorry, I was asleep – we were rather late last night – we had company. Hullo, Celia! I'm Gina Timble.'

'Are you Mrs Timble?'

'Not exactly, but you could say so. I've your kids here.'

'I know. Can I come and collect them?'

'Well, if they've surfaced. You come along, Celia. We don't stand on ceremony.'

'Gina, listen, I have to tell my children something serious.'

'What's that?'

'Their father's dead.'

'Oh hell! You can't get much more serious than that. Sorry, Celia! You come and tell them – I'll see they're up and making sense.'

'Where do you live?'

The address was distant enough to persuade Celia to drive there. She wanted to reach her children before they were involved in breakfast and preparing for school and college. The Timble home was in a terrace, grubbier than the other houses, and with a faded flyer in the downstairs front window advertising CND.

She rang the doorbell. Gina Timble opened the door – long dyed red hair with black roots showing through and a knee-length sloppy joe jersey.

'Come along in, Celia,' she said.

She led the way towards the kitchen, from

which sounds of young voices and laughter issued.

Celia wanted to see the children alone, in a quiet room or in the car, but was too late to stop Gina, and found herself in the doorway of the kitchen.

They were sitting at the kitchen table, Charlotte, Paul, Jane Timble, an overweight girl of Charlotte's age with long hair in little plaits Afro-style and a bold expression, and a bearded and bespectacled youth. They all stared at Celia as the chat and laughter subsided. Gina pointed at the girl and said: 'Meet my daughter Jane,' and, pointing at the youth, 'that's Jane's boyfriend – we call him Tinker.' She added for Jane and Tinker's benefit, indicating the figure in the doorway: 'Here's Celia.' She had clearly not warned Charlotte and Paul that their mother was coming to collect them.

Celia said hullo and Charlotte piped up defiantly: 'Dad gave us permission' – meaning that Alan had allowed them to stay with the Timbles.

Paul said: 'I'm going to school' – his obstinate tone suggesting that he was not going anywhere with his mother.

Jane, interfering in a nasty tone of voice, said to Celia: 'And Charlotte and me, we're going to college' – reinforcing Paul's message.

Gina had the grace to address both Sturridges. 'You'd better speak to your ma out here.'

They exchanged glances and got to their feet protestingly. Celia retreated towards the front door and waited for them.

Charlotte, approaching, demanded: 'What is it now?'

Celia said: 'I'm sad to have to tell you your father died yesterday, last night.'

Neither of the children spoke.

Celia continued: 'I'll be in the car for the next ten minutes. Do come and join me. Then I'll be at home until lunchtime. In the afternoon I'll have to arrange the funeral with or without your help. I'll be back at home round about five.'

She opened the door and closed it behind her. Five minutes later Paul emerged from the house followed by Charlotte in tears supported by Jane Timble. Paul sat in the front passenger seat, Charlotte sobbed in the back seat.

'What happened?' Paul asked in his rough way.

'He died of a heart attack. He had fallen over in Paradise Street. He was brought into St Hugh's. I was there.'

'Did you see him?'

'Oh yes. I was with him, but he was unconscious.'

'You didn't let us know.'

'It was the middle of the night, and he was dead. If you'd like to see him, I'll drive you to St Hugh's. He's still in the Cold Room at the hospital.'

As an afterthought she said: 'I might have woken you and let you know if you'd been at home.'

There was no further conversation in the car.

In The Homestead Celia had to telephone Paul's school – Jane Timble had undertaken to inform their college why Charlotte was otherwise engaged. She made her children drinks of hot chocolate and carried the mugs on a tray into the sitting-room, where Charlotte was drying her eyes on the sofa and Paul sat frowning beside her. She was not thanked, and perched on a hard chair facing them – she felt like a criminal brought to justice.

'Did you have a row with Dad?' Charlotte asked.

Celia was taken aback – a raw nerve had been touched.

'What makes you think that?'

'Dad said you'd be cross with him when you got back from being with Grandfather, you'd be cross because he'd told us all about Anthony.'

'It wasn't a row – I'd planned to tell you myself – when I was over Anthony's death, and you were older and I had the strength. I was upset because I was afraid you were upset, and I was right, because you ran away and gave me the cold shoulder. I'm full of remorse for having reproached him – but none of us will ever know why he had the heart attack. His heart was in poor shape, he'd been threatened with heart trouble for ages.'

Paul barged in.

'Dad told us he'd had a pain in his heart ever since you put Anthony in that sort of prison.'

'Do you know what autism is, Paul?' she inquired.

223

'Not much,' he said.

'Do you, Charlotte?'

'I know it's an illness, not a crime,' she said.

Celia had another question.

'You've jumped to the conclusion that he should have been brought up with you, in the family, as if he were any boy, haven't you?'

'Well, yes, all right – we think so, and Jane who's studying psychology does, and Gina Trimble does too – and Gina rang a doctor friend of hers who said the same thing, that autistic children only have a chance of recovering if they're treated as one of a family, like an ordinary person.'

'Anthony wasn't ordinary. He was exceptional in every way from birth onwards. You don't remember – as I hoped – as your father and I both hoped, and why we took the necessary steps.'

Paul said: 'Dad wouldn't have had a pain in his heart for years if he'd done away with Anthony.'

Celia replied: 'Please mind your English, Paul – I won't be called a murderer even by mistake.'

'Sorry!'

'Far from being a murderer, I arrived at the decision to have Anthony treated elsewhere mainly to make sure that you or your sister or both of you and all of us wouldn't be murdered.'

Charlotte burst out, 'That isn't true,' and Paul chimed in: 'Dad didn't say that!'

'I feared it. I had reason to fear it. I didn't tell your father. I tried to spare him, and you and you, and Anthony, who might have been locked up for life in an asylum if he'd committed a terrible crime without meaning to – I tried to spare you all, and, in line with my worst expectations that made me secretive, you're not sparing me.'

'What did he do wrong?' Paul asked.

She described the French burn within inches of his jugular vein; the blow on Jake Thornton's nose; the death of Timmy the canary; the drama in the car. She described Anthony's speechlessness, which was never cured, and the malice of his character in childhood. She described his escapism, that he could not be allowed freedom of movement in an unfettered environment. She described his eating habits and his digestion.

'I couldn't manage him at home,' she said.

'Dad said the place he was in was expensive. You could have paid carers instead,' Charlotte pointed out.

'What carers?' Celia asked. 'A carer who was qualified to look after autistic cases, who had nerves of steel and could run as fast as Anthony, would have cost a terrific lot, and he or she would have needed a replacement for time off and holidays, and really a night nurse was also required. I had a husband and two "ordinary" children to see to, and would have had to work even harder to earn money to pay carers than I was working – four days a week of nursing – to keep Anthony at Orchard Grange, where he had a team of experts to care for him and myself seeing that he came to no harm.'

'Dad didn't like Orchard Grange,' Charlotte objected.

225

'I know he had reservations. Do you know how often he saw Anthony there? Once! Your father was a good man, you should be proud of him, and I was privileged to have been his wife. He was clever and dependable. But he couldn't cope with Anthony at all, he was defeated by the sadness of the Anthony problem, which you both seem to think you could have solved by carrying on as if it didn't exist.'

'Gina Timble –' Charlotte began, but Celia interrupted her.

'Tell me more about your Timbles – where's Mr Timble?'

After a pause Paul volunteered: 'There isn't one.'

'What do you mean?'

'Jane hasn't got a father.'

'Oh dear! Does Gina work?'

'She does sculpture.'

'What are her sculptures like?'

'She sticks bones together.'

'Whose bones?'

Paul had to laugh.

'Animal bones,' he replied.

'Where does she get them?'

'They're the bones of meat that people eat, cutlet bones and things like that, she gets some from the butcher.'

'What do her sculptures look like?'

'I don't know.'

Charlotte took over.

'They're interesting, and Gina's brilliant – you're not to run her down, Ma.'

'And you're eighteen, your friends are your business now, but I don't think it's right that you should quote your friends and their opinions against me and mine.'

'Gina wouldn't have chucked him out of his home.'

'How do you know that? Why do you say that? You may like Gina and her daughter, but they lead untidy lives and think they can save the world. Anthony in the Timbles' care wouldn't have lasted long. Who would have changed his nappies and washed them? He would have escaped and got lost or been run over. He didn't understand danger. He couldn't have joined in high-falutin talk. He wouldn't have appreciated sculptures of old bones.'

Charlotte persisted.

'He would have got love from Gina.'

'No, Charlotte. That's wrong. What Anthony got wasn't sentimental twaddle and impracticality, it was my life for seventeen years, and my mourning until I die. I do apologise for correcting you. And I do hate explaining myself and justifying myself and trying to, I hate it in others and hate it most when I'm the person doing it. But I must remind you and Paul that you were the cause of Anthony being in Orchard Grange. The proof of the pudding of my arrangements for Anthony is your objecting to them. You are so unmarked by the fate of Anthony, I mean his illness, that you think you could have grown up with him as you did without him. You enjoyed normality because your father and I sheltered

227

you from abnormality. Don't flinch at my words, don't! Anthony did recover probably as much as possible in the Orchard. His anguish and jangling cries and irrational actions – all that subsided towards the end. I felt that he became a remarkable person in spite of his handicaps, and that he and I were close at the end. At least I admired him as well as loving him. That's all I can say about Anthony now, in the way I've had to say it, defensively – I rest my case, in legal language. This afternoon I'll go along to Coopers the undertakers to fix up your father's funeral, leaving here at three o'clock – I hope you'll come with me. There's food in the fridge for lunch and dinner. Meanwhile I'll be upstairs, thinking of your dear father, your dear brother and even my mother, and telephoning your grandfather and Mr Carter, your father's boss.'

In her bedroom, that had also been Alan's, she broke down. She was ashamed of having argued with Charlotte and Paul, and entertained a fear that she had presented them with some-thing else not to forgive her for. But she rang her father, who comforted her for every reason and said he would motor over immediately. She also rang Mr Carter, who was sorry to hear the sad news and said he would bring Alan's will across on the day of the funeral.

Bernard Farr arrived in time for lunch, the family ate together, then walked to Cooper's. An armistice if not peace broke out. The children returned to their educational establishments. Celia and her father came to the conclusion that The

Homestead would be too big for Celia to live in alone, when Charlotte and Paul moved out as children do, and even before then.

The funeral was followed by a modest wake at The Homestead. After it, Bernard had to return to Thanet Steps, and Mr Carter produced Alan's will and read it to Celia and her two children. It was simple, Alan's estate was shared out in quarters between his wife and his three children. Celia as Anthony's next of kin would inherit his share.

A month passed. Charlotte and Paul were nicer to their mother. Twice Charlotte cried on Celia's shoulder, once for her father, once for her brother, and both times by way of a partial apology for the awful scene on the morning after the night in the Timbles' house. Charlotte had changed, was losing her puppy-fat and promising to be quite pretty even though her face and her nose would always be on the long side. She was actually a soft-hearted girl, and perhaps the hard rude streak she had shown was attributable to a mixture of the anti-maternal phase of teenage females and the influence of the troublesome Timbles.

The obstinate streak in Paul resembled Charlotte's unexpectedly hard one. Celia wondered if they had inherited a version of her own determination. Paul at seventeen was handsome and good at games, which she hoped would compensate for his bad results in exams. He too had atoned – with a filial hug or two – for his part in the trial of his mother. He was somewhat inarticulate, but not a bad boy, Celia reflected.

She herself was neither happy nor well, physically well, in this period. She spoke to Dot and Con on the telephone: they told her she was run down, not surprisingly, and bereaved, and needed a long idle holiday, such as she had not had since she divorced Owen Pennant. Her father offered her time at Thanet Steps, alternatively an extended visit from himself. Edward Speed urged her to come back to help at The Orchard. She lay on her bed, drowsing in the day, worrying at night and often crying.

An unpleasant conversation with her children had a revivifying effect. It occurred about a month after Alan's death. The family of three was finishing supper in the kitchen of The Homestead. The children exchanged a conspiratorial glance, and Charlotte spoke up.

'Ma, are you thinking of moving from here into a smaller house?'

'I was, yes,' Celia answered.

'Are you still thinking about it?'

'Not seriously, not for the moment, no.'

'Is Dad's will in action yet?'

'I don't know. I suppose so. Why?'

'Well, if it is, Paul and I own half the house, don't we?'

'What are you getting at, Charlotte?'

'We'd like to sell it.'

'Would you? What for? Where would we live?' Paul joined in.

'The Homestead's awfully valuable,' he said.

'Is it? How do you know that?'

230

'The father of a friend at school, he's an estate agent, and he told me it's worth a fortune.'

'He can't be right. We didn't pay anything like a fortune for it.'

'There's a property company after all the houses round about, Tom's father says, and we're part of the plan.'

'Fancy that!'

'Anyway, Tom's father says the house is worth a lot, and we should test the market.'

'Does he now! You sound like an estate agent yourself. I will think again about moving; but I'm attached to our Homestead. Your father and I sold our flats and pooled our resources to buy it, and it has sentimental value.'

Charlotte said: 'Dad put it in his will, all of it, I mean.'

'Yes, but he and I bought it together.'

'He thought it was his, legally, though.'

'Am I right to be worried by the way you're talking, you're both talking? I'm not sure I like it. I own half the house both historically and legally, because of Anthony's share, so it can't be sold without my agreement. I'm sorry if I'm disappointing you. Shall we change the subject?'

Paul said: 'Anthony's share should belong to us.'

'What?'

Charlotte explained: 'Dad left three quarters of his estate to his children.'

'I see,' Celia commented, and a momentary silence fell.

Her heart sank in the interval. Belatedly, she

231

sensed animosity towards herself in these exchanges. But she knew she must not let anyone make a scene, she must not be involved in a scene about money, money of all things, in which she had never been interested.

'Can I have a little time to ponder your suggestions?' she asked.

'Of course you can,' Paul said.

Charlotte said: 'We're pondering, too – no more than that.'

'It's all right – you've made some good points – we'll work things out to everyone's satisfaction, I hope – I'm sure.'

The children thanked her, and she shooed them out of the kitchen to watch TV while she washed up the dishes.

In the next few days she made telephone calls. She spoke at some length to her father, also to Dot and Con. She spoke to Edward Speed, who drew on his experience of predicaments like hers to console her yet again by saying: 'Many of the troubles associated with autistic children can be traced to their siblings.' She spoke to friends at St Hugh's and Orchard Grange. And she had dealings with Carter Johnssen and her bank manager.

She and Charlotte and Paul were not getting on too badly when she wrote them this letter: 'Dearest Charlotte and Paul, You are the two people I love best in the world, but you have grown up now, you're adults, so I'm leaving you to make your own way and do as you please. I shall have left when you read this letter. I don't

232

have to go, and I'm not going for fear that you would wish to be rid of me. No hard feelings on my side, only gratitude for the years you've spent with me. For my shortcomings, sorry! For our differences over Anthony, sorry! When we meet again, if we meet again, provided we're all willing to meet, I hope that you may have come round to seeing that we were caught in the trap of Anthony's illness, the whole family was. The trap was baited by choices, and every choice was harmful – my choice was harmful in your opinion, yours would have been harmful in mine. Anthony might have benefited from being at home, on the other hand I heard at Orchard Grange of a boy who was admitted because his brothers had tried to kill him. Your father's choice was not to choose, which I could not sanction because Anthony had to be removed before you two really noticed he had gone. My choice was meant to be protective of all concerned, believe it or not.

'Years do blunt the sharp edges of harm. I pray for that to happen, before we do harm to one another.

'Your destiny is in your own hands from now on – a truism, also a truth. I have signed over a power of attorney to you two – it means you own The Homestead and its contents and your father's money, and you will receive some compensation from my waiving my right to his pension from Carter Johnssen. I am taking with me only the money in my personal account that holds my earnings from nursing. Your GranFarr knows what I'm doing, Dot Tyler and Con Thornton know – you will find telephone numbers in my address book, but I cannot guarantee that anyone will be able to contact me for the time being.

'My decision has been arrived at calmly. I would say my motives are twofold. I love you and want to give you time to decide whether or not to love me, and secondly because I believe in happiness, not misery. My ambition always was to devote myself entirely, without reservation, to the person or people I care for, and, according to my standards of happiness, I'm lucky to have realised it. Agreed, I could never be exactly joyful because of Anthony, but I knew he was well looked after and kept in reasonable health, and I believe he was as happy as possible, I have reasons to believe he was latterly, and that you two and even your father were happier than might have been the case. I dare to claim that I did turn great misery into at least a little happiness.

'I'm leaving now to give you the chance to search for whatever you think happiness is made of, and to seek it once more for myself. Happiness isn't everything, the modern cult of happiness is awfully selfish and usually counterproductive. We nonetheless do owe it to life to try to find and create something better than misery.

'Goodbye, good luck, and I hope it isn't too corny to add, *au revoir.*'